Fairy War

E.J. Graham

Winnipeg, Canada

Developmental editor: Craig Gibb
Proofreader: Francisco Feliciano

Published May 2022 by Deep Hearts YA, an imprint of Deep Desires Press and Story Perfect Inc.

Deep Hearts YA
PO Box 51053 Tyndall Park
Winnipeg, Manitoba R2X 3B0
Canada

Visit deepheartsya.com for more great reads.

To Ellie for being there when it was hard,
Sarah for putting up with me pitching books to her,
and my family or always believing in me.

Fairy War

Chapter 1

"Help me…please…"

I looked up, puzzled at the sound of a voice in the seemingly-empty garden. Nothing appeared out of place, however, and there was certainly no sign of the source of the voice—if that's even what I'd heard—so, assuming I must have been daydreaming, I returned to my digging, hoping I'd eventually find the right depth to bury the seeds.

"Please…not much…time…running out…"

There it was again—that same voice, coming from somewhere nearby, somewhere close to where I was crouching.

I paused, listening intently.

Although my head told me to ignore whatever it was I'd heard, my curiosity had most definitely been piqued, and I started walking over toward where I thought the voice had come from. As I went, I saw something that made me freeze in my tracks: just visible between two rows of flowers was a strange blue glow that grew fainter as I watched. Reluctant to turn back, I approached the patch cautiously, getting close enough to view the source of the light.

At first, I wasn't sure I could believe my own eyes.

There, lying in the undergrowth, was what appeared to be a fairy. It was weak, and clearly in dire need of help, but it could never be mistaken for anything else. A dark blue cloak was drawn around its body, a glint of silver armor just visible beneath the folds of the tiny outfit. Poking out from its shoulders was the top of a set of wings, made of the smallest feathers I'd ever set eyes upon. I don't pretend to be an animal expert, but I was fairly sure there were no animals in the world that looked like that.

I shook my head, taking a deep breath. This just wasn't possible, was it? This had to be my mind playing tricks on me, surely?

"You're confused, aren't you?" it said weakly. I nodded in response, unsure of how to react to these events—I was used to the strangest thing in my life being Mr. Robins down the road walking a turtle into town. "I'll explain," it continued, "I promise…just get me some water. I don't have long to talk."

For a moment I considered telling my parents—despite being a teenager who was most definitely not averse to keeping secrets—but two things stopped me: firstly, my father was at work and my mother was painting in the attic, with strict orders not to be disturbed (I wasn't keen on interrupting her after what happened last time). Secondly, my parents would never believe there was a fairy in our garden anyway, which I could more than understand. After all, I'd heard the stories about other children who'd claimed they'd seen fairies, and their fate really didn't bear thinking about.

"Stay here, I'll be back in a moment," I said, although in that state it was clear the fairy wasn't going anywhere.

I walked quickly back up to the house, checking no one was in the kitchen before carefully pouring a glass of water; the last thing I needed was someone sneaking up behind me and asking what I was doing. Then, having made sure my mum was still blissfully unaware of the events occurring within our garden, I headed back outside to find the fairy.

It was in exactly the same position as before, but its glow had faded even more. I quickly held the glass to its mouth, hoping it wouldn't drown, and was pleased to see the glow returning slightly as it drank. After a few moments the little creature stood up, though it barely reached the rim of the glass.

Still struggling for the right words to say in this scenario, I hesitantly asked, "So…you're a…a…"

"Fairy? You're right, I am," it said, watching my puzzlement with a slight smile. "Prince Naarin, one of the last of my kind."

"The last of your kind?" I asked, staring at the little Prince. "I don't understand…"

The fairy paused, clearly thinking deeply about how to answer the question. As he pondered, he paced in the undergrowth before turning to face me, a serious look on his features once again. "In the last few months, have you noticed anything change?" he asked eventually.

"Change?" I asked, frowning. "What do you mean?"

"I'm…not sure," the fairy admitted. "I'm not sure what the signs in your world would be exactly." He paused for a moment, thinking. "Have you seen anything in your world changing, people acting differently…perhaps seeing strange things that aren't there?"

I almost laughed. "Not that I…wait…actually, there was one thing," I said, thinking back to the night before. "I was looking in my mirror yesterday when I could've sworn I saw something over my shoulder." I shrugged. "I don't know what it was, and when I turned to look there was nothing there."

For a moment the fairy said nothing, although after a bit of fidgeting he announced, "I'm not sure how to explain it by myself, but what you're seeing are the effects of a great war between the forces of light and dark."

"A war?" I repeated, frowning. "I haven't seen anything on the news; they'd have reported—"

"No," the fairy said, shaking his head. "This isn't a human war. You're only seeing its effects because the forces of light are losing…badly…and that's not the worst news, I'm afraid." The tiny creature took a deep breath, something that sounded like a high-pitched sneeze. "If we can't turn the tide of this war, it won't just be a problem for the fairies; the humans will lose too. That's why I need your help."

I bit my lip as I tried to think of some response. In all honesty, I was dumbstruck. "But why come to me?" I asked eventually. "You could go to the U.S., the president could help you stop this, I'm sure. I'm just a sixteen-year-old boy from some boring town on the south coast of the Isle of Wight. What help can I possibly give you?"

"You don't understand," the fairy said, a slight tinge of anger in his voice now. He paused for a moment, evidently trying to calm himself down. "I assume you've heard the stories of people who've claimed to see fairies before?"

"Yeah," I said, wondering where this was going.

"Well, we've tried to contact your kind before—I can't even guess how many times—but each time the person we found vanished afterward. My coming to you is one of our last chances to try and change things for the better."

"No pressure then," I mumbled under my breath, trying not to focus on the word "vanished". "But I still don't get it. Why me? What have I ever done that could possibly make you think I can help?"

"It's not what you've done, Clint, it's what you *can* do…what I'm afraid to say you'll *have* to do before this war is over."

"How do you know my name?" I asked, a slight chill running through me. "And I still don't get what you think I can do."

"The children we've tried to contact all had one thing in common, Clint: their birthday. *Your* birthday. All children born on that day have one thing no one else in this world has." The creature paused, peering up at me with his wide eyes. "I don't mean to pressure you, but…well…you could be the difference between us winning and *everyone* losing."

For a moment I had no idea what to say. I was completely dumbstruck again, both by the creature in front of me and by what he was saying. I could scarcely believe what I was seeing, just a foot away, let alone all this stuff about a war. Could he really be telling the truth?

Just then, my thoughts were interrupted by a shout from the kitchen. "Clint, I'm making lunch! Do you want something to eat?"

My heart sank. Whatever my mother had been painting in the attic had either been finished or put aside for a break, meaning she was no longer occupied by her artwork. I knew I couldn't take Naarin inside to show her, but I also knew I had to reply to her before she got suspicious and decided to investigate what I was doing.

Suddenly, I had a thought. "Nah, I'm going to see Mickey and Crystal; I found this spider I think they'd like," I called back, hoping her fear of spiders would halt any thoughts of further questions. It would definitely stop her from coming outside.

Now my only problem was finding some way of getting a fairy out through my house without anyone noticing what it was.

"If my memory serves me correctly, there's an old toolbox in your shed. You could take me out of your house in that," Naarin suggested, as though he'd been reading my mind.

"But…" I said hesitantly, "your…glow…"

"Leave me to worry about my glow; you worry about my transport."

I nodded before running over to the shed, keeping half an eye on the back door to check my mum was still inside. So far, so good. After finding the key in the little plant pot on the ground, I opened the shed, grabbed the toolbox, and locked the door again. It was only as I was putting the key back that I wondered how my mysterious companion could have known there was a toolbox in there, but I decided it was probably best not to keep asking questions. I wasn't sure I wanted to know all the answers, anyway.

When I returned to Naarin, I found that his glow had all but vanished. "How did you do that?" I asked, before stopping myself. "Sorry, you don't have to answer that if you don't want to. Come on, get in—we don't have much time."

Naarin clambered inside, taking a few moments to make himself comfortable in the enclosed space. After checking he was okay, I closed the lid and headed inside the house, hoping there'd be no awkward questions.

"How long are you going to be, darling?" my mother asked, not even looking at me as she did the washing up. "I was wondering when to make dinner."

"I'll text when I'm done. Should only be an hour or two, I hope."

She didn't reply to that, though I wasn't surprised; my parents only seemed interested in me whenever my school report was sent to them. Sometimes that was bad, but other times—like now—it was exactly what I needed.

I headed out of the house and then abruptly stopped on the pavement, opening the toolbox. As I lifted the lid, the fairy took a big gulp of air.

"Remind me to never get in one of your boxes ever

again," he said, stretching out his wings. "Did you really just lie to your parents about where you were going?"

"Yeah," I said, shrugging. "I don't think my mum would react too well to me saying I'm taking a fairy for a walk."

A smile crossed the Prince's face, but he managed to hold in his laughter for the time being. "You've lied to them before, haven't you? About...other things you've seen? When you saw me, you looked less shocked than I expected you to be," he pointed out.

"Well...I've seen things before, yes...like, there was something at my birth; I keep having a recurring dream about it."

Naarin nodded. "About a small white figure standing by your mother's bed, as if it was guarding you?"

"Yes," I said, frowning. "How did you know that? Was it you?"

"No," said the Prince, shaking his head. "What you saw was what the fairies call a Watcher. All the children we've been searching for all these years saw a Watcher too."

"All of them? How many of them were there? And what are the Watchers?"

"There were thirty of you," the Prince replied from inside the toolbox, "all born in the same year but with differing birthdays, and there are thirty Watchers...or, at least, there were. They've slowly been dying out, I'm sorry to say. Only four of them now remain."

I was about to ask a question when I realized what I must look like—if anyone saw me out here, they'd surely be wondering why I was talking to myself, or worse, my toolbox. Quickly, I headed down the pavement toward the furthest house on the street.

"Where are we going?" the Prince asked. "You have the advantage over me in your world; I've never been here before today."

"To my friends' house," I replied. "Don't worry, they can be trusted. They won't freak out when they see you and they don't get along with their parents, so they won't rat on us."

"I didn't think they would," Naarin said, barely flinching. "I knew about them already, thanks to others of my kind. You see, they're two of the other three kids we're seeking, hence why I was in the area. I wasn't just here to find you alone."

I stopped for a second, wondering whether I should ask him more questions, but as I could see our neighbours giving me strange looks through their windows, I decided it was best for us to move on as quickly as possible.

I still hadn't got much further along to my friends' house when I saw them coming toward me, both of them smiling. Crystal ran up and hugged me—forcing me to move the box to stop her crushing it unintentionally—while over her shoulder Mickey mouthed something to me, forcing me to suppress a laugh.

"Hey, Clint, we're just off to the skate park, you want to come with us?" Crystal asked, eyeing the toolbox suspiciously. "And where are you going with that thing? You going to build a shed?"

Mickey was forced to stifle a giggle.

"What?" I asked. "No, of course not. Look, I can't explain—or, at least, I can't out here, anyway."

"Why not?" Mickey asked. "It's not like it's a treasure chest or anything... is it?" He laughed.

"Clint, I advise we get out of sight now," Naarin said, his voice carrying clearly from inside the toolbox. "Something's coming this way!"

Mickey and Crystal looked at me, their mouths open in shock, and realising we had no time to waste, I ducked behind the wall of my garden, quickly signalling for the others to follow.

"What is—" Mickey started asking, then stopped as I put a finger to my lips.

Poking my head around the corner of the wall, I froze at the sight across the street. A figure in a suit was standing opposite my house, but that wasn't what had caught my attention; at first, I thought I was looking at his shadow, until I realised it seemed far too solid and unconnected to his body to be one. But if it wasn't his shadow, then what...?

Just then I felt something land on my shoulder, and when I turned my head I saw Naarin sitting there, watching the scene as well.

"This isn't good at all," Naarin said. "I'd heard rumors of this, but I assumed that was all they were." He shook his tiny head as he looked at the figure in the suit.

"What is it?" I asked quietly, worrying my mother might hear our conversation from the house. "What's that thing with him?"

"The same thing you glimpsed in your mirror that

night," Naarin whispered. "It doesn't have a name you could understand, but the closest translation is 'Nightstalker'. You almost never see them during the day."

I frowned. "If that's true then why is this one out during the day?"

"It's a scout, Clint," the Prince explained. "The enemy is hunting you down. By the looks of it, someone's helping them too."

I felt Crystal tap me on the shoulder. "Clint...does one of you two want to tell us what the hell is going on? 'Cause I'm pretty sure that's a fairy you're talking to."

Naarin shook his head. "Not now, there will be time to explain."

I sat there in stunned silence for a moment, trying to get my head around everything. Then, realising that the wall we were hiding behind gave us little or no cover, I bit my lip, searching for some way out of the situation without being spotted by the figure in the suit, this "Nightstalker".

"We have to go, Clint; we aren't safe here any longer," Naarin said, his gaze unwavering from the scene opposite. "If he doesn't see you soon, he'll come toward the house, and I can guarantee you don't want to be here when that happens."

"But my parents," I protested, "they have to be warned!"

"That would achieve nothing aside from getting you captured," Naarin said, his voice remarkably calm considering the circumstances. "Don't worry—the Nightstalker won't kill them; they aren't who he wants."

"But are you sure?" I asked, the panic clear in my voice. "How can you know for certain?"

"Listen to me," Naarin said rather sternly, looking me straight in the eyes. "Staying here and getting caught by them will not help you, the fairies, or anyone else, for that matter. You want to know why the Watchers are dying? The kids—ones just like you—are vanishing without a trace. *All* of the missing kids told their parents what they saw, and they were never seen again. I'm afraid you can't trust adults, *any* adults."

"But…they're…" I trailed off, unable to say anything else.

"I know," Naarin said, a little more gently this time. "This war has claimed the lives of both my parents already. If we're lucky we may yet be able to save yours. Now come with me and I'll take you to my sister; she can explain this better than I."

I nodded, Mickey and Crystal pausing for a moment before also nodding. As I edged behind the shrubs, heading toward the gate that led toward the back garden, I asked, "Where do we go? Do we need to go to the bottom of my garden or something? Go find the nearest oak tree and look for a hidden door?"

"You have a strange idea of fairies," Naarin replied, a smirk on his face. "The few fairies that once lived in those places are long gone. We don't trust humans any longer."

I didn't answer, amazed at how a member of a race who seemed to feel such hatred for my kind was so determined to help us, but after what I'd witnessed in front of my house, I wasn't about to complain too loudly. And I wasn't about to waste any more time.

As we snuck into the back garden, I took a second to glance over at the house, feeling relieved to see my mother facing away from the window. Naarin was no longer hidden away, and I didn't fancy trying to explain to anyone—let alone my parents—who the strange, winged figure perched on my shoulder was.

We continued, and as we headed toward the back gate of my garden, we tried to stay as quiet as possible.

"Clint," Mickey said as he walked alongside me, "is there any point in me asking you what's going on here?"

"You don't want to know," I said. "Not yet, anyway." I turned to peer at the creature on my shoulder. "Naarin, I sure hope you know where we're going because none of us do."

"Through there," Naarin said, pointing to the gate. "Hopefully they'll waste a few minutes searching through the house, giving us the time we need."

At his words I started to walk even quicker, and when we reached the gate Naarin hopped off my shoulder for a moment. As I reached down to open the latch, however, I suddenly hit a problem. "Uh, Naarin," I said quietly, "we might need to rethink our strategy. The gate won't open, even though I could've sworn it was unlocked this morning. And climbing over isn't a great idea unless we want to hurt ourselves."

I crouched down to allow Naarin to lean toward the gate, a puzzled look crossing his face as he went to touch it. It looked as though he was being pushed back by some invisible force, and his look of puzzlement soon changed to one of panic.

"We were too slow," he whispered, "it knows we're here!" He reached toward the gate again, but the exact same thing happened. "Clint, leave this to me; you aren't ready to face a Nightstalker."

"But if he's threatening my family, you can't expect me to just stand aside and do nothing," I pointed out, sounding far braver than I felt. "Let me fight him!"

Naarin was about to answer when I turned to look at the house, seeing something that made my blood run cold: from where we were standing, we had a straight-on view of the kitchen window, through which I could see the man from the street talking to my mother. As the figure approached the doorway, I realised I was frozen to the spot, though Naarin had no trouble moving; slowly and steadily, Naarin drew a small but deadly-looking blade out from under his clothing.

"Clint, what's happening?" Crystal asked, biting her lip. "I don't like this; if this is a joke then I'm definitely *not* laughing."

I wanted to reply, to try and comfort her, but what could I say? I was terrified myself, and in that moment, I was completely unable to speak.

The door opened, and I watched wide-eyed as the Nightstalker moved toward us. This was the first time I'd caught a close glimpse of it, and I jumped as I saw a pair of ice-blue eyes just visible amidst the dark shadow that I assumed was its body. The figure had claws at the ends of its long arms, and although they didn't appear solid, they still looked nasty enough for me to know I should avoid them at all costs.

"Out of my way, fairy, the boy is mine!" the creature snarled, its deep voice dripping with menace. "I'll take his friends too; I'll be richly rewarded for capturing three Chosen in one raid."

"They're going nowhere with you," Naarin replied, an almost eerie sense of calm emanating from him. I realized, to my surprise, that he'd grown to human size. "I'm taking

them from here and soon we'll be out of your grasp. Your magic cannot harm me!"

"Oh really?" the creature laughed. "If that were true you'd be through the gate and long gone by now—your magic is too weak to stop me, fool. You can't honestly believe these…these *halflings*…will threaten us?" He was sneering at us now, making my blood boil despite my fear.

"You underestimate their powers, Nightstalker," Naarin said, still seeming remarkably calm. "You should watch that—it may be your undoing one day." He took a step toward the Nightstalker, his weapon raised high and poised to strike at any moment. "If you want a real fight, then face me. Let's go, right now."

As the Nightstalker got closer Naarin hopped off my shoulder and walked forwards, as though preparing for battle. I watched the two circling each other, noticing with a jolt that Naarin still seemed weak from his earlier efforts.

I needed to do something, even if I wasn't sure what I *could* do.

After frantically looking around the garden, I picked

up a loose brick that had been lying nearby, the weight of it feeling good in my hands. Then, waiting until I could get a clear throw, I launched it at the Nightstalker. Though the brick passed straight through him—which was a strange sight to behold—it grabbed his attention long enough to make him turn away from Naarin.

"I was going to kill the fairy first, but I suppose it doesn't matter what order you die in," it snarled as it moved towards me, forcing me to back away slightly.

"What are you doing, Clint?" Naarin hissed nervously. "Believe me, you *really* don't want to pick this fight."

I was beginning to think he might have a point, and I backed into the gate, hopelessly feeling along the wood for some way of opening it as the creature got nearer and nearer.

I had no luck, and before I knew what I was doing, I shouted, "You won't take me without a fight!" as I swung a punch at the creature. Somehow, I managed to force it back, but not before one of its claws had slashed me across my right hand. I immediately started feeling dizzy, and I fought to stay upright as I glimpsed the creature heading back towards the house.

"I've won, Prince, now watch the end of your last hope!" I heard it laugh faintly as I fell to my knees.

Something wasn't right. No, something was very, very wrong.

Naarin rushed over to me, quickly followed by Mickey and Crystal. "Clint, stay with me, we'll get you help," Naarin said, but I could barely hear him as I slumped to the ground.

The last thing I saw before I blacked out was Crystal's face, covered in tears.

Chapter 2

"You shouldn't have brought him here. How do you know you weren't followed?"

"What choice did I have? If I hadn't brought him here, they would have got him. This is the only safe place for them now."

My head was swimming as I tried to make sense of the conversation I could just about hear through my drowsiness. The second voice was unmistakably Prince Naarin's, of that I was certain, and while the other voice was female, it was far too high-pitched to be Crystal's.

Suddenly I felt a weight on my stomach, as though a pair of hands were running across my skin, and a very small pair of hands at that. I was just beginning to wonder if I was having some bizarre dream when the voices continued.

"He's lucky you did bring him here; Nightstalker poison is deadly to humans…"

I stiffened upon hearing those words; at least, I would have if I could move. I was still too scared to do anything.

"I hunt creatures like this for a living," Naarin said, a note of frustration in his voice. "You aren't telling me anything I don't know already. Can you save him or not?"

"You really need to ask me that?" the female voice said. She laughed. "I could heal him with my eyes closed."

Suddenly, I felt as if water was being flushed through my entire body, cleaning out any nasty substances that might have been lurking within, and thinking I could no longer ignore what was happening around me, I opened my eyes for the first time since the attack.

I immediately found myself looking into the face of a red-headed girl, whose ice-blue eyes shone in the sunlight filtering through the trees around us, a faint smile crossing her face as she noticed I was watching her.

"Crystal..." I said, confused at the presence of this strange figure.

"Here I am," she said, appearing to my right, a look of relief spreading across her face. "I was...we were worried you wouldn't make it."

"What happened?" I asked, trying to think back. "I only have a vague memory of the attack."

"What happened," the red-headed girl said sternly, "is your friends and that fool of a Prince may have just saved your life. You should at least thank them for it."

"Wait...who are you?" I asked, now feeling a lot less drowsy.

As my eyes adjusted to the light, I realised that what I'd assumed to be a human girl was in fact a fairy, shorter and slimmer than Naarin, dressed in long red robes that stretched far enough down to hide her feet. The surface of her wings seemed to glitter with diamonds, shining even brighter because of the amount of sunlight in the clearing. She had a little pouch slung over one shoulder, with some kind of plant poking out of the top, and over her other shoulder there rested a small bow. She was standing on my chest and peering at me intently.

"This is Nikkela, one of my kind's best healers," Naarin said, out of my eyesight but still easily audible. "By luck she was out foraging when we brought you here."

Nikkela rolled her eyes. "What Naarin forgets to tell you is that I'm one of the few remaining healers we have left," she uttered. "Most of the others are apprentices, trying to learn from me. If I die before they're ready, then our kind is doomed."

As Naarin's light form landed on my chest next to Nikkela, he visibly winced at the last statement, causing Nikkela's smile to widen at his obvious discomfort. As his wings twitched slightly, I could just about make out a tear on the very tip of one wing. A war wound from earlier.

"Anyone want to fill me in as to where we are?" I asked, looking around me. "I mean, this doesn't look like my back garden anymore…unless someone's planted a load of trees while I was asleep."

"Wow, you didn't tell me our great hero was a comedian too, Naarin; these guys really are multi-talented." The female fairy laughed rather sarcastically. "We're in Parkhurst Forest, thankfully a part of it few visitors ever enter."

"How come?" I asked, sitting up slightly and making the two fairies flutter gracefully down to the ground. "This doesn't look particularly different to any other part of the forest. Same old boring surroundings: trees, trees, and more trees."

"Oh, the naivety of *inhimillien*," Naarin laughed. "You see what we *want* you to see. But what if you look closer, Clint? You may find that your surroundings are a little… different…to how you imagined."

I did as he asked, but at first all I saw were the same trees I'd glimpsed before, with nothing particularly extraordinary about them and nothing to suggest they were anything other than normal, everyday trees. Confused, I was just about to laugh off the Prince's claim when I noticed something around me had, indeed, altered; what looked like tiny Christmas lights were now strung between the trees, with other lights flying quickly between them. I could also hear strange but beautiful music wafting through the air, although I was finding it difficult to figure out from which direction it was coming. The other thing I noticed was the smell of freshly cooked food—the origin of which was somewhere close by—making my mouth water (which was no surprise considering I hadn't eaten anything for at least half a day). It smelled almost like the roast dinner my mother cooked, but there was another fragrance I couldn't identify that drifted through the forest with it.

"They weren't there…"

"Just now?" Naarin asked. "They've been here all the time, Clint. Humans don't see our kind because they don't believe we're there, and any who do happen to glimpse us convince themselves it's just a trick of the light, alcohol…

anything to deny the truth. Children see us because you've refused to give up on our world; you've always believed we were there somewhere."

I tried to take all that in, but my head was still feeling a little fuzzy. "What is this place?" I asked. "I mean, it's clearly more than just some random corner of a forest."

"It's a place of celebration," Nikkela answered cheerfully. "There is a great feast this night, hence the lights you see between the trees. This is one of the few chances we have to be happy." Her smile faded then. "In fact…this may be our last chance."

"I don't understand," Mickey said finally, having remained silent so far. "You make it sound like you're dying."

"We are," Naarin said firmly. "The fairy race is being picked off one by one; as each person in this world who still believes in us dies, the darker beings of this world grow stronger as we grow weaker. This may be our last chance to feel joy and happiness." He was smiling at me, but I could tell it was a smile filled with sadness.

As I sat there, trying to get my head around everything, I watched the fairies decorating the forest, stringing up baubles and trinkets that looked almost the size of some of the fairies carrying them. Some of the objects were so big they required two fairies to carry them.

Mickey and Crystal were quiet, watching me closely, and as I turned to Naarin and Nikkela, I bit my lip while I tried to find the right words. "You said that without us the fairy race will die out?" I asked.

Naarin nodded. "I hate to put so much pressure on you, but yes."

"Then tell us what we need to do," I said forcefully. "If I understand properly, you want us to join this fight?"

"You haven't even begun to understand what's happening here, child," Nikkela responded angrily, her good mood seemingly gone. "It isn't your kind facing extinction." I saw her drawing the short blade in her belt as she spoke, making me back away slightly.

"Stop this!" Naarin exclaimed, jumping between us quickly. "This will help no one, humans *or* fairies. Nikkela, you're right, his kind aren't facing extinction—not *yet*, anyway."

"What do you mean 'yet'?" Crystal asked. "You can't keep me and Mickey out of this; it affects us as well."

I was just about to answer her when Naarin put his hand up, signalling for me to keep silent. He paused for a moment—apparently trying to consider how he should phrase what he was about to say without terrifying my friends—and then started his explanation. "The only reason creatures like the Nightstalker rarely attack humans is because the fairy race forms a line of defence around your kind; it's a combination of what soldiers we can spare from the defence of our own cities, and numerous curses and magical barriers." He paused. "However, this defence is only as strong as us and our magical powers. The less of us there are…"

"The weaker the defences against them are," Mickey finished, an expression of realisation slowly crossing his face. I could see the same look in Crystal's eyes.

"Exactly," Nikkela said, the anger having now vanished from her voice—at least, temporarily. "If we die then the human race are *turvaton sorsa* against these beasts."

"But we can stop them," I insisted, "we have all our technology—"

"If your technology was capable of stopping them," Naarin said calmly, "then why would you need us to protect you? You would have no hope against them, and the Nightstalkers are only the advanced guard of what you would face; there are far darker beings in this world than gremlins or poltergeists, believe me."

All three of us had been shocked into silence, and for a moment even the two fairies didn't speak, allowing us to hear the sounds of the forest all around us as we contemplated their words.

Suddenly, I noticed what sounded like birdsong wafting through the trees nearby, a faint smile crossing my face as I realized I was listening to music, although I couldn't work out what kind of musical instrument was being played. I saw a faint smile cross Naarin's face too as he realized I could hear it.

"You have a choice," he said, watching me closely. "We can visit our city—the Shadow Glade—immediately, so you can speak to my sister, or we can stay here and join in the celebration first, before going to the city. I would not suggest it but for the fact that none of you have eaten for a while, and I assume you don't want to speak to a royal on empty stomachs?"

We all laughed then—including Nikkela—as at that

moment my stomach growled loudly, emphasizing the Prince's point. In fact, it was so loud that even the fairies who were busy decorating the clearing looked around at the noise. I could feel heat spreading through my cheeks, embarrassed at so many eyes watching me so intently.

"I promise there will be nothing in the food to poison you," Nikkela said, giggling slightly, although that thought hadn't even occurred to me. "If we wanted you dead, you wouldn't even have made it into this clearing."

I stood up slowly, wincing slightly as I felt a twitch of pain shoot up my leg. "That's nice to know," I replied as Crystal put her arm around my shoulder to keep me steady.

"Careful, Clint, you're not a superhero. You need time to recover," she said sternly, raising her eyebrows slightly as Naarin's stern glare forced Mickey to stifle a giggle.

"This way everyone," Nikkela said, sounding more relaxed now than any of the others in our small group. "I'm afraid the Queen cannot join us, as other…events…have distracted her. Actually, she's rarely seen by anyone but her family and her inner circle nowadays."

"Why?" Mickey asked as we picked our way through the trees towards the source of the music. "King Tristan appears in public with regularity."

"Yes, however, I doubt your King faces threats to his life whenever he leaves the safety of your cities. Or does he?" Naarin was clearly unsurprised as he saw us shake our heads in response. "There was a time when fairies could be safe in the human world—as long as we avoided predators—but that was at least three or four generations ago now." He sighed. "Fairies are meant to live in beautiful cities above ground, but now we're often forced to travel through underground tunnels."

"What do you fear so much about the outside world?" I asked. "I mean, you told us most adults can't even see you."

"They can't," he agreed, "but you humans aren't what scare us. The Nightstalkers are a mostly limited threat, rarely appearing during daylight hours, and few fairies will venture out during the hours of the night. However, the enemy has other beings to call upon, and unfortunately it includes…well, some of our own."

"Fairies are fighting *against* you?" I asked, aghast.

"Yes," stated Nikkela grimly. "Unfortunately, there's one thing that can really tempt our kind: they were offered the chance to survive once the rest of us have fallen. Those who took the offer have changed beyond recognition— gone are the bright colors and the wish to protect nature, replacing them with darker colors and a far darker magic. For all the power we have, it's just no match for the powers the fallen fairies wield—even our Queen can only just barely defeat their magic."

I didn't reply to this speech, the reality of what was occurring really beginning to dawn on me with every revelation from Naarin and Nikkela. There was just so much to take in, and apparently so little time in which to do it. My head was spinning.

As we rounded a large tree trunk I was hit suddenly by a bright light, flooding the clearing we'd just entered. At first, I assumed it was sunlight, until I realised it was almost night-time and the sun had therefore almost set.

Shielding my eyes with my right arm, I soon discovered the source of the illumination: hanging from every visible branch were several brightly-lit lanterns, casting more light on the surroundings than sunlight would ever have managed through these trees, and shedding a warm glow on the scene of revelry that filled the floor of the clearing. As I took everything in, I began to worry where we were going to sit, as most of the clearing seemed to have been filled with fairies of all sizes and colors.

"Sit over here with us," Naarin said, pointing to the biggest table of all that had been set up at the far end of the clearing. "It's reserved for the leaders of our kind, plus any special guests."

"Special guests? Us?" I asked, unable to believe what I was hearing. "But we're nobodies—just a bunch of kids from Ventnor! We don't deserve any special treatment."

"Good to see some humans still have modesty," Nikkela said with a hint of sarcasm, winking at Naarin. "You could help save our world, I think that counts as something deserving of special treatment."

I saw Crystal turn bright red then, dipping her head as if trying to hide her reaction from the others, although a hint of a smile on Naarin's face told me he'd also got a glimpse.

As we approached the table, I studied the others who were already sitting there. Most of the fairies in the clearing were dressed in what could have passed for human clothes—if they were increased in size—but these fairies were dressed in more unusual clothing than the others.

The female fairies (or what appeared to be female fairies, anyway) were dressed in long, elegant robes, which in some cases even covered their hands. The garments came in every color of the rainbow, with one of the fairy's dresses seeming to shimmer and change colors every few moments. It was mesmerizing to watch.

"That's my sister, Niana," Naarin said quietly, noticing what had drawn my attention so intently. "She's the next in line to the throne."

"The dress," I whispered, "how does…"

"It change colours like that?" the Prince finished. "What you see is a dying art within our kind; a skill that only a handful can understand, let alone manage to achieve. Basically, the fabric is enchanted by a spell—one that doesn't translate into any human language. The theory, although you'd have to ask my sister to get a straight answer, is that it reflects the mood of those around it, or something like that." Naarin shrugged, and noticing the look of puzzlement on my face, added, "Hey, I'm a warrior, I don't meddle in magic. Male fairies have magical skills too, but there are now so few male fairies left that we've become dependent on the females' skills."

"How can there be so few male fairies?" Crystal enquired.

"Well, there are a mixture of reasons, Crystal but two main ones," Naarin explained. "Firstly, this war has taken a heavy toll; we've long since stopped counting how many have lost their lives. And secondly, a great many before the war started—and a worrying number since—have switched sides: they've joined the *varjo*."

I looked back at the dress in wonder, enchanted by the effects of the spell, though I was brought abruptly back to the present when I lost my balance and nearly fell over. Glancing down I saw two full plates of food being carried by a rather irritated-looking fairy, who hurried on quickly when he saw the Prince standing next to me, while he muttered something under his breath.

We finally reached the table, Niana smiling and standing up to greet us as we approached, and nodding to Naarin as they made eye contact.

"Welcome, friends," she said, still smiling at us, "it has been…many…lifetimes since a human last took a place at a fairy celebration. Please, take seats next to me." She pointed to three empty seats.

I smiled back. "It's almost as if…"

"You were expected," said a fairy sitting on Niana's left. He had an eyepatch over one eye and many scars on his face. "You think the enemy are the only ones who've been watching you? Naarin's a good tracker, but he's not *that* good."

"Thanks for the vote of confidence," Naarin replied, shaking his head. "That is General Arcturus, the most experienced soldier in our army. He's been fighting since…well, for longer than he cares to mention."

I heard a stifled laugh from Mickey behind me, and when turned to look at him I saw his cheeks were bright red—he'd just realised half the clearing was watching him closely.

We walked to our seats, Niana insisting I take the seat next to her, and I sat down politely. At least sitting next to her allowed me to take a closer look at the strange, multi-colored nature of her clothing. It was at this moment I also noticed she had the most amazing purple eyes, a shade I'd never seen aside from contact lenses. When I realized she could tell I was staring at her, I turned toward the table, embarrassed.

I'd expected to see tiny portions of food to go along with the tiny fairies and was exceptionally glad when I realized everything seemed human-sized. At least, that's what I'd assumed. In actual fact, our surroundings had grown much larger, an effect that made me feel more than a little dizzy; with my vision blurring, I nearly fell off my chair, but thankfully I was rescued by Prince Naarin just in time, who put his arm around me before I could fall. He was now the same size as me, something I'd only just noticed. What on earth was going on?

"My apologies," Niana spoke, turning toward me as I sat upright again. "My brother should have warned you about this. You may have noticed there are certain…size differences…between us, which would make it difficult for you to enter our city."

"But then how…"

"A spell," Niana answered. "It shrinks any human that steps within the borders of this clearing to our size, allowing easier interaction. "It also allows you to enter our city, otherwise you would be too large. It has another use too; should one of your kind attempt to attack us, you make far easier targets at our size. In the time it would take for them to adjust to the spell's effects they would be surrounded."

"Oh, you could've warned us though," Mickey said. "I'm sure I've had nightmares about stuff like this happening to me."

"It's been a long time since any human has made their way inside this clearing," Naarin said in hushed tones. "Most of your kind don't even know this place exists. We forgot to warn you about it because no one alive today has ever needed to give that warning to anyone."

"It's okay," I answered, though I was still feeling rather strange about the whole thing. One look at the food, however, pushed all that from my mind.

I dug into the dishes in front of me, starting with some meat that looked vaguely like chicken, although it tasked unlike any meat I'd ever eaten before. I smiled instantly, an amazing sensation filling my body as I swallowed the delicious food. It felt like I'd eaten far too many sweets at once, and when I began to feel slightly light-headed, I took a sip from the glass of water next to my plate.

"Be careful, the food has certain…properties, shall we say…that might have an interesting effect on humans," Naarin chuckled "We have to fly; we can hardly make the food heavy, can we? Light food helps us, although it isn't necessarily going to fill growing humans." He smiled apologetically.

"This food is great though," Crystal said between mouthfuls. "I'd love to eat this every day. Your meals must be amazing!"

"If only that were true," Niana responded with a tinge of sadness in her voice. "Finding food like this is a rarity nowadays, so it is only served on occasions like this. Few fairies even leave the Shadow Glade anymore, beyond soldiers or our hunters."

"Because of the enemy?" I asked, watching Niana's face closely.

"Not just that, Clint—there are many threats to creatures our size," Niana said, staring straight back at me. "Humans may not be able to see us, but that doesn't mean the rest of the natural world cannot. Foxes, cats…even badgers have eaten fairies before. They're probably not aware of what we are, most likely they just see us as another meal."

I almost choked on the piece of meat I was eating, imagining a giant fox or badger looming down at me.

"Why don't you just use your magic?" Mickey asked, with only a hint of sarcasm in his voice. "You use it to hide this clearing from humans…stopping animals from attacking you should be easy."

"You humans are the most arrogant creatures in the world," Arcturus uttered angrily. "If our magic could protect us then don't you think we would have used it already? We can barely protect our own city with what magic we have left!"

I was about to open my mouth to speak—as was Mickey, by the looks of it—when Naarin held up a hand to silence us. I noticed with some alarm that his other hand was gripping his sword as he scanned the edge of the clearing, and I could see that same alarm on the faces of Niana and Arcturus.

"Niana, get the others to the tunnels," Naarin

commanded. "Arcturus, get every soldier you have lined up on the edge of the clearing. We have company heading straight toward us, and I don't think they're bearing gifts."

"What about us?" I asked, watching the fairies following their Prince's orders, seeming amazingly calm considering the situation. I could feel my heart pounding in my chest. "Should we go with the others?"

"No," Naarin said, his face suddenly taking on a grimmer appearance. "Stay with me and Arcturus. Even if you can't fight you can help carry our wounded back to the tunnels. Just remember to stick with me or the General— you'll be in less danger that way."

I ducked down—with Crystal and Mickey doing the same either side of me—and looked at the clearing intently. I could see fairies spreading across the whole of our side of the clearing, taking cover behind anything they could find rather than taking to the air. each of them carrying either a bow and arrow or a short sword, all of them wearing glimmering suits of armor. I also noticed that some of the soldiers wore face paint, designed to camouflage them amidst the leaves. It was only watching these silent maneuvers that made me notice the fact that grass and plants that were barely taller than my feet ordinarily were now more like trees towering above me.

As I looked back toward where the feast tables stood, now empty, I suddenly felt very uncomfortable in the eerie silence that had surrounded us.

"Something isn't right, I agree," Naarin said, clearly sensing my unease. "They're here, but I don't understand why they're staying hidden. After all, they…"

Arcturus put his hand up, silencing the Prince and pointing quickly toward the far edge of the clearing, where I spotted what had caught the General's attention: two dark shapes had landed at the end of the table furthest from us, apparently inspecting the empty plates that had been left behind. One of them was clearly a fairy, though he was dressed in darker-colored clothes than the fairies with which I'd been feasting. His hair was white, falling past his shoulders in a tangled mess and looking as if it hadn't been brushed for many weeks. This contrasted curiously with the red eyes I could see shining in the center of his face, with no noticeable eyelashes whatsoever. Buckled in his belt was a deadly-looking knife, sharpened to a point like a spike.

The other creature was far stranger in appearance, a long black cloak hiding all but its claw-like hands, just visible as they emerged from his sleeves. For a moment, I could have sworn I saw some kind of aura around the creature, or perhaps a shadow, but it was too difficult to tell for sure. Unlike the silvery wings that were visible on the fairy, the other creature had no obvious method of flight, a fact that, judging by the looks on their faces, seemed to have puzzled Naarin and Arcturus as well.

"They were here before, I swear," I heard the fairy in the dark clothes say as he pushed plates off the table. "How could they have escaped so quickly?"

"The same way they always do, Miraeck," the strange figure responded, sounding angry. "As long as those tunnels remain hidden from us, they'll always have an escape route." He grunted. "They come from your own city of birth—can you not track them?"

"If they were that easy to track then we wouldn't be standing in an empty clearing now, would we?" the fairy snarled. "We're not the only ones not keeping their bargain. Your anti-magic abilities were meant to help us attack the Shadow Glade and yet its defences still stand," he pointed out.

"We're powerful," the creature replied, "but your former Queen's magic is beyond ours. We will give you the city, but we need time." He grunted again. "Or, of course,

you could just waste your lives in a fruitless attempt to attack the city with its defences still standing."

"Fine, we wait," the fairy responded, grimacing visibly at the creature's last comment. "This search is pointless, Karal'el; they are long gone by now. We should leave this place."

The creature nodded, and as the two of them turned around and the fairy took off, my attention was drawn to the other creature's method of flight. Emerging from within the folds of its cloak were two huge bat-like wings, propelling the creature off the ground and out of sight.

My mouth hung agape as I stared at the place where the two figures had stood just moments before.

"So, the stories about them are true," Arcturus uttered under his breath. He turned to face Naarin. "We had best go and see your sister, Prince, for I fear we have more problems than we realized."

Chapter 3

When we reached the entrance to the tunnel network, I was still worried by the reaction of the General, unsure as to what it was I'd been watching in the clearing.

At first, I could see nothing more than the same forest clearing we'd been walking through, surrounded by plants and tree roots, with the sound of birds circling far above our heads, and I was just about to ask how we could find the tunnels when I noticed something: a nearby tree root, though it was different to the others. Whereas most of it was the same dark brown of the rest of the tree trunk, one part of the root was a much lighter brown, with veins that travelled vertically, rather than diagonally like the others.

"There's a door," Crystal uttered in surprise, pointing to the barely visible door handle poking out from the lighter section of the root. "How did we not see that before?"

"If the door was that easy to find then the enemy would have discovered our tunnels in no time at all," Arcturus said, his voice barely hiding his frustration.

"You're only here because you're our guests; the guardians would have killed you in an instant if you were intruders."

As he said these rather worrying words he pointed up into the tree, where I could just about catch a glimpse of some fairies, only identifiable from the occasional glint of their wings between the leaves. They were draped in long, dark green cloaks, which matched their surroundings, and they were armed with an assortment of weapons, some with short bows and others with sharpened spears of varying sizes, some intended to be thrown. They had them trained on us.

"Don't worry, Clint," Naarin whispered, "I'm a fairy Prince; they won't attack without me or Arcturus telling them first."

I just hoped Naarin knew what he was talking about.

Slowly and cautiously, we walked toward the door, the fairies around me keeping a hand on their weapons as Naarin opened the door and signaled for us to enter. I ducked as I walked through the doorway, still finding my height too large for the entrance despite my new fairy-esque size.

I gasped as I took my first glimpse at the interior, surprised to see that lanterns were strung on both sides of the tunnel, with what looked like small fireflies winging their way between each light. As each firefly touched the flames of the lanterns, their brightness seemed to increase even further. The tunnel stretched out in front of us in a straight line for as far as the eye could see, undisturbed by any other fairies or animals.

"Those creatures are sprites," Naarin explained, having

noticed my curious gaze. "At least I think that's the word you have for them. We call them menninkäinen, and they're weakening, just like us. They do, however, do the one task we can't; we barely have enough time to gather food for our meals, never mind keep the tunnels lit."

We walked through the tunnel in silence, Crystal watching the sprites intently as we passed each lantern. Every now and then we saw murals that had been painted on the walls, most of them depicting scenes of battle with fairies and other creatures I didn't recognize, in landscapes ranging from deserts to forests, and even what appeared to be human cities. They were fascinating.

"There were times in the past when humans and fairies existed side by side," Naarin explained, having noticed my interest. "It is the greatest tragedy that the friendship our races had is now all but gone." He walked a bit further along the tunnel and then paused, pointing to one of the murals that hung above a cluster of four especially bright lanterns. "This is what Shadow Glade once looked like. I thought you would especially like to view this."

I looked at the mural—which was far larger than any of the other images—to see a huge city depicted in the paint. It seemed to gleam as if it had been built from diamonds or some other gemstone, and it was surrounded on all sides by tall flowers and trees. A large wall enclosed the city, within which were mostly small buildings, except for the huge structure at the center.

"That is the seat of the royal family," Arcturus said, a hint of awe in his voice. "I could attempt to describe the beauty of it, but you can only fully understand if you see it for yourself. It is one of the few visually appealing things left in our realm."

"How old are these paintings?" Mickey asked dreamily, as though the mural had put him into some kind of trance. "These look like they're fading slightly."

"Even the newest is many decades old; we have neither the skills nor the magic to create these anymore," said Arcturus sadly. "The number of fairies who could even create this has dwindled greatly."

I sighed as I stared at the city. My mother—being an amateur painter, herself—had taken me to numerous museums and art galleries while I was growing up, and had consequently taught me to appreciate art, so the prospect of these paintings being lost forever disturbed me greatly. If the fairies died out and so did these, what would be left of their own world?

We stood there for a second longer before Naarin and Arcturus set off down the tunnel again, the three of us following close behind.

As we made our way further into the tunnels the passage became much taller and wider, meaning we could walk together in a group of five, side by side. In the darkness, with no way to tell the time, it seemed as though we were walking for hours, and just as I was about to ask how much further we had to travel I saw two figures standing at the end of the tunnel. As we approached, I realised they were two fairies, leaning on spears and carrying shields that had small spikes at the bottom. Their clothes were mostly hidden under long, dusty brown cloaks.

They crossed spears as we reached them, blocking our way, and they peered at me, Crystal, and Mickey with an air of suspicion.

"What are you doing bringing their kind down here?" one of the guards asked the fairies as he moved toward me, his sword drawn. "Defending this place is difficult enough without helping the enemy find a way in!"

"They're with me," Naarin replied, stepping in front of us and causing the guards to visibly cower at the sight of royalty. "Do you think I would be stupid enough to *help* our enemy? I'm taking them to the Queen on urgent business."

"It's their fault we're even *in* this position," the other guard spat at us, a look of pure hatred in his eyes. "Why are we asking them for help? The days of humans and fairies living together are long gone."

"It's that kind of *typera* attitude that will be our downfall, soldier," Arcturus replied, rushing forward and forcefully pinning the guard against the wall. "These children can help us, and we *will* need their help. Now let us pass."

The guards reluctantly stepped aside, opening the door as we passed between them, the looks of distrust still clearly visible on their faces.

Crystal—who'd gone on ahead of me—gasped as she saw what was on the other side of the doorway, and as I rushed to keep up, my jaw dropped.

In front of us, laid out amongst the endless blades of grass and spreading as far as the eye could see, was a magnificent city that seemed just as colorful and mesmerising as the dress the princess had been wearing. None of the houses were just one plain shade; each displayed a whole variety of colors from golden yellow to every imaginable shade of green and purple. Fairies could be seen both walking through the streets and flying through the air, adding to the rainbow effect. I could hear hundreds of chattering voices—almost loud enough to ensure I couldn't hear myself think—with the faint sound of metal clashing against metal only just audible above all the voices.

"They're still discussing the events of the picnic," Naarin said, smiling slightly at the cacophony. "They're mostly annoyed they never got to finish their meal, I expect." He laughed. "Right, that's where we want to get to," he added, pointing above the roofs at the largest building in the whole area, on top of which a spire rose up, circled by vines and other plants, giving it a tree-like appearance. Windows dotted the outer surface of the spire, glittering as if parts of the structure had been clad with mirrors.

"I thought Buckingham Palace looked impressive, but this beats it hands down," Mickey said, his voice full of awe. "I'm guessing that's your family's house, then?"

"You're half right," the Prince said. "That is the Queen's residence. The male royals are only allowed inside when they need to speak to the ruler—they have a smaller but no less impressive building just behind the Queen's tower. You three are lucky; the last human to enter its interior was…well, before even Arcturus was born."

Naarin dodged a light-hearted clip round the ear from a rather rueful-looking Arcturus. "I meant that in the nicest possible way, General. Honest."

We all stood laughing for a moment—even the General was grinning slightly—but our giggles were soon stopped by the sound of a bell ringing out across the city. In an instant the streets were emptied as doors slammed shut all around us, and within seconds the city had fallen deathly silent.

"What was that all about?" I asked Naarin. "Is it some kind of curfew?"

The Prince put a finger to his lips and then pointed to a nearby building, signaling that we should take cover.

As we ducked around the wall, I realised Arcturus and the soldiers had remained where they were; they were pointing their bows at the sky, arrows already notched.

Looking up, I saw what had caused the panic. More creatures like the one I'd seen in the clearing were attempting to break through the barrier that surrounded the city. Their faces were almost human—except for their long fangs—and they looked angry. Very angry.

Each attack produced a shower of sparks across the surface of the shield, each shower being accompanied by a burst of bright light. Every now and then the sparks would temporarily illuminate the creatures' faces, causing both me and Crystal to gasp out loud.

After five more minutes of these pointless attacks the creatures withdrew again, the fairy soldiers lowering their bows as we stepped out from our hiding place.

"This is not good," Naarin uttered, a note of panic in

his voice. "We'd better hope those defences can hold; if they break through, our troubles will get far worse."

"What do you mean?" Crystal asked. "What are those things?"

"We call them Fenrir," Arcturus replied. "We don't know where they originated from, but they're one of our most dangerous foes. They have an ability to dampen magic: all but the most powerful fairies' powers have proved useless against them."

"And they use them against the barrier because…"

"The barrier is formed from a magic more powerful than any ordinary fairies could ever hope to wield," Naarin explained. "The royal family are more powerful than even the fallen fairies, but as our powers weaken, so too does the barrier. Unless we can regain our strength it's only a matter of time before they break through, and if they do, all hell will break loose." He paused for a moment, shaking his head slightly. "Well, we'd better get to the palace now; we've wasted enough time already."

As we headed up the main street, I caught glimpses of many faces staring out from behind brightly-colored curtains, as well as the occasional fairy child poking their head over the windowsill to try and sneak a peek.

The further we walked, the more patrols I could see circling the area, each of them heavily armed. They seemed far less interested in us than the others, barely noticing our passage through the streets, except to bow to the two fairies.

Finally, we reached the doorway to the palace, an ornately decorated entrance that was covered in images of nature at its wildest—fairies were visible, flying alongside ravens and larger birds, with some even riding them like horses, while other animals scurried through the undergrowth. As I looked closer, I realised there were two parts to the image on either side of the door—they each showed the same place, but the two scenes were entirely different. On closer inspection, they bore only a handful of similarities.

"What are those carvings?" I asked, entranced by the images.

"They're intended to show how this city has changed over the years," Naarin answered. "It was one of the last pieces of artwork ever created by our species. On the left is the city as it was before it became the Shadow Glade, when it was known as...well, translated into your language its name was Forest of Mirrors, a name I cannot even begin to explain to you. Back then, animals of all kinds could traverse this valley without troubling or threatening us."

"Even humans?"

"Even your kind," Naarin agreed. "Back then nature and mankind existed together peacefully, but the moment your cities expanded, everything began to change."

"And the other side?" I asked, looking back at the door.

"The other side of the doorway shows the Shadow Glade again, but the way the city is nowadays. Now we have to shut out nature, as most animals pose just as much threat to my kind as any of our enemy's forces. If a human was ever to find a way to breach our defences, it would signal the destruction of this city."

I stared again at the other side of the door, seeing the far darker tone that seemed to emanate from the images. Where the opposite door was covered in scenes of beauty and nature, this side was decorated with images of war, both against creatures I recognized and creatures I definitely didn't.

"We should enter," Arcturus said, breaking the temporary silence that had fallen over our group. "The Queen is not a fan of being made to wait, especially if her brother is involved."

Mickey sniggered, but soon stopped when Crystal gave him a frosty glare.

Once Naarin had knocked on the door, we entered a bustling room full of fairies standing in small groups. I recognized many of them from the feast, and most of them were dressed in long, elaborate dresses. The male fairies were mostly formally dressed in dark tunics, and there was also the occasional soldier dotted around, signaled by the weapons sheathed in their belt. The majority of the fairies were far too engrossed in their own conversations to pay any attention to our entrance, and those who did seemed to look at us with disdain. It wasn't exactly a warm welcome.

Just then, a door at the far end of the room opened and an elaborately dressed male fairy entered carrying a large scroll. He cleared his throat, instantly gaining the attention of everyone in the room, and then made his announcement. "Her majesty, Queen Nareena, ruler of the fairy realm and its surrounding territories."

As he stepped aside, everyone in the room, apart from me and my friends, got down on one knee, and as a gasp rippled through the waiting fairies, Naarin hurriedly signaled to us to do the same.

A tall fairy, larger than even Naarin or Arcturus, walked into the room then. He was dressed in elaborate golden armor and a light blue cloak, with a sword, that had diamonds gleaming in its handle, tucked into his belt. The armor also seemed to have small gems embedded in it, a mixture of moonstones and rubies from what I could tell, creating small glimmers of light all across its surface.

As he stepped aside a smaller female fairy appeared, and while at first, I thought she was Niana, I soon realised she was only similar-looking. This fairy had a silver crown covered with diamonds, rubies, and other gems I couldn't recognise perched on her head. Her hair was even more golden than the male fairy's armor, and she had beautiful jade green eyes, glimmering with the light from the lanterns that were hung about the room, which added an even more magical air to her appearance. Her jade green dress gleamed from what I assumed was fairy dust.

She waved her hand and the other fairies returned to their groups.

"She looks…amazing," I said, watching as she disappeared into the mass of fairies.

"Is that other fairy her husband?" Mickey asked Naarin, his gaze fixed in the same place mine had been.

"He wishes," Arcturus responded, laughing slightly.

"No, that is the royal bodyguard; he goes by the name of Nightshade, although I've never figured out why. He's the only male fairy allowed within her inner chambers...well, until she finds herself a husband, anyway."

"I'm sure they don't need every detail of my family's love lives, General," Niana said, appearing suddenly. She turned to me, a smile on her face. "My sister's had numerous suitors, Clint, but not one of them has been appealing enough for her. She's always been a little... picky...when it comes to men."

"I know a few girls like that too," I replied, laughing, and I was glad when Niana joined in.

At that moment a band started playing in some distant corner of the room, the music floating over to us, and immediately the fairies began pairing up—except for Naarin, Arcturus, Mickey, and Crystal, who went to one side of the room—leaving me and Niana alone.

I blushed slightly, barely able to make eye contact with her but unsure of where else to look. "Uh...would you like to..."

"Dance? I would love to," she replied, taking my hand. Seeing the look of worry in my eyes, she smiled slightly. "Come on, I'll show you how to dance. Just don't let go of my hand at any point and don't go off dancing with someone else."

"Why, are you jealous?" I asked, before realising how that might sound. "Sorry, I shouldn't have said that."

"Don't worry," she replied, flicking a strand of hair from her eyes and nodding at the other dancers. "This always happens after a feast, and it's always followed by a *very* long sleep."

With that we began dancing around the room, just about managing to avoid bumping into the other dancers, her eyes watching me all the time. I was distracted by the occasional glance in our direction from the other fairies, but mostly I was able to keep up. It was pretty wonderful.

We remained like this for what seemed like an hour at least, but when I felt a firm hand on my shoulder, I saw the smile vanish from Niana's face.

"Clint, her majesty wishes to speak to you," a rather harsh voice said from behind my back.

I turned around to find Nightshade looking down at me, his gauntleted hand resting firmly on my shoulder. I felt a slight panic, worried as to why the Queen wished to speak to me, a feeling Nightshade seemed to sense.

"Don't worry, she's in the best mood I have seen her in for a long time," he added, smiling and making me feel—slightly—more at ease.

He headed off through the crowd, going toward the door of the Queen's chambers, and I followed behind, Niana at my side. I turned around briefly to see if I could spot the others, but the crowd was too packed to see them. I was surprised, therefore, when I reached the doorway to find all four of my group waiting for me, including Mickey and Crystal.

Having entered the Queen's chambers a few seconds before, Nightshade emerged again, smiling slightly as he announced, "You may all enter now, but please bear in mind that she's not well, so try not to cause her any stress."

We all nodded in response, and as I stepped inside my jaw almost dropped, amazed at the vision in front of me.

The room was large enough that the ceiling was hidden in shadow, although the occasional light could be seen flitting back and forth above our heads. The walls, rather than being painted or covered in wallpaper, had been left as bare wood to give the room a more mystical air. The only things that interrupted the otherwise natural appearance were the various paintings that were hung up, each one depicting a different fairy, the crowns on their heads indicating they were past rulers. I was amazed to notice that only two male fairies were among the paintings, both of whom were similar in appearance to Naarin.

At the far end of the room was a stunning ruby-encrusted throne, upon which the Queen was sitting, her eyes closed as if she was sleeping. Standing next to her was an elderly fairy with short, silvery hair, dressed in a long black cloak.

We were ushered further into the room, and moments later I was standing right in front of the impressive throne.

"My apologies that we did not meet in better times, Clint," Nareena said quietly as she opened her eyes, her voice wavering a little. "I have long dreamed of meeting humans; I am probably one of the few fairies who do not fear you, whether or not others would admit it openly." She stood up slowly, standing unsteadily for a moment before being forced to accept the support of her helper. She looked at the same time both my age and incredibly old, her colorful hair and eyes in stark contrast to the deep wrinkles that covered her face. She took my hand, amazing me with her strong handshake. "Do not underestimate the strength of the fairies," she said, a glimmer of a smile on her face. "We are stronger than we appear."

"M'lady," Arcturus said, bowing. "I'm afraid the situation has deteriorated even further today. It appears the Fenrir have become more…opportunistic."

Her smile immediately dropped. "Explain."

"If we hadn't moved quickly enough, they would have attacked our feast, or even traced us back to the tunnels. I fear they will find a way through our defences soon."

"Then it is as I suspected," Nareena said sadly, sitting back down on her throne. "I have long feared this day would come." She focused on me again. "Clint, there is one thing Arcturus and my brother have not told you about the Fenrir. It is a secret known only to a few of our kind."

"What do you mean?" I asked, bewildered.

"Clint, the Fenrir…well, there is a reason they understand fairy magic so well. They *are* fairies."

"Those things are fairies?" Crystal asked, her eyes darting between me and the Queen, who seemed to have shrunk suddenly.

"They *were* fairies," Arcturus corrected. "The story of how they changed is such a shameful moment in our past that the royal family have hidden it for nearly three centuries. Do you want me to explain, your majesty?"

The Queen nodded, signaling for us to sit on a set of chairs that had been lined up in front of the throne.

Naarin walked back to the door, poking his head out briefly into the dancehall before returning and taking the only remaining seat. Arcturus bit his lip, tightening and loosening his grip on his sword before clearing his throat and beginning the story.

"Many years ago, when fairies still walked among your kind, there was a group of fairies who began to notice…a change. Why it happened we're still not sure, but we call it the shrinking. Eventually humans began to lose faith in us, though it happened so slowly at first that the loss of magic was missed by most. Some, however, *did* notice."

"The Fenrir?" I asked without thinking, immediately feeling embarrassed at having called out so suddenly.

"Yes, although they weren't called that at the time. Their leader was one of our then ruler's closest confidants." Arcturus pointed to one of the few portraits that showed a non-royal. This fairy had long emerald-green hair, and eyes that seemed to glow with an unnatural light; it almost felt as though his eyes were staring into my soul.

It was only after a few seconds of looking that something dawned on me: he looked almost identical to Naarin, in facial features at least.

"That is our ancestor," the Queen uttered quietly, having noticed the look in my eyes. "My family has not ruled this city forever; we gained the throne barely a generation after these events. Our ancestor Karan saw the beginnings of the evil's encroachment into human lands, and attempted to warn the King of what he'd seen. Unfortunately, at that point we were filled with the same arrogance you humans have now: he refused to listen to the advice."

"But then how did they become those bat…things?" I asked, trying to keep track of everything.

"The ruling class at the time believed his group were trying to stir up trouble, so they decided to use them as a warning to any who would question their rule. They were cursed—at first most believed it was so they could never return to the city, but it changed them. If we'd realized they were trying to help us in time we may have been able to save them, but now they are beyond rescue." She stared into the distance, a little sadly.

"I don't understand," Crystal said suddenly. "Why are they fighting against you if they're your own kind? If you're right, they were exiled before the enemy had any foothold in our world."

"Unfortunately, they only joined our enemy's ranks for one reason: to gain revenge for the great wrong they believe was done to them. It is a mistake the fairy race has been paying for ever since."

At that, every single occupant of the room fell silent, and I took the opportunity to try and sort through my thoughts—I was struggling to believe what I was being told.

Suddenly, Nightshade leaned in to whisper something to the Queen, who stared into the far corner of the room as she listened. With that, Nightshade left, and once her guard had gone she said nothing for a good few seconds.

Eventually, she stood up again. "Arcturus, I need you to go prepare the soldiers. Don't tell them why, just inform them it is my order. Clint, Crystal, Mickey, you need to follow me; there is something I must show you."

Arcturus bowed, his cloak drifting through the air as he turned around and headed toward the doorway.

Nareena signaled for us to follow her, leading us over to a smaller door that had strange writing above its frame. It read as *kielletty*, with leaves and branches that seemed to trace their way down to the floor of the room.

Nareena reached for something at her neck, taking off a necklace with a rusty-looking key attached, and when she unlocked and opened the door, I could only see pitch-black coming from the other side—that was, until she waved her hand and a whole host of candles lit up the room.

"This is the hidden archive of the Shadow Glade," Nareena said in hushed tones.

I peered inside. An elderly fairy was sitting at a desk, hunched over and writing in a large book, quietly uttering words in a language I could not understand. He didn't even flinch as we entered.

"He can hear us; he just likes to ignore people unless he finds them interesting," the Queen said, walking up to him and gently tapped him on the shoulder.

"Huh…oh, your majesty," he said, smiling as he saw his Queen. He stopped when he saw us, turning to close the book in which he'd been writing. "I knew you'd want to see it eventually; you had better follow me."

Picking up a lantern, he led us further into the room, and as we walked, I looked at the books lining the shelves on either side; alongside what I assumed were fairy books, I saw some human ones too. These were really old books, covered in layers and layers of dust.

Suddenly, I realised I could hear someone breathing nearby, though it was too far away for it to be any of the group.

Just then the light of the lantern fell on a bed hidden in an alcove, whose occupant caused gasps among the whole group. The figure lying on the bed was neither fairy nor Fenrir, but appeared to be a creature stuck somewhere in between. Its fairy-like face hid two fangs, and its wings already looked more like a bat's than the delicate wings of a fairy. It tried to sit up on its elbows to look at us, and failing, it sagged back onto the bed with a groan. As it did I realized he was so emaciated I could see his ribs through his skin. The wings also seemed like they might break at a moment's notice.

"This is Eilith," Nareena announced, waving a hand and making several chairs appear out of the floor. We all sat down, though rather uncertainly. "I do not know whether he was spared because my ancestor realized her error in time to show mercy to one of her former kin, or whether Eilith somehow resisted the curse which afflicted so many others, but he has lived like this for longer than many within this city have lived at all."

"I would wish death upon no one," Crystal said, her eyes moist with tears, "but he's clearly suffering—is there nothing you can do to help? Surely you have something that could ease his pain at the very least?"

"My curse gave me knowledge few fairies possess," Eilith said, coughing. "I was the one who warned the former Queen that the Watchers' children were in danger. I am doomed to see hints of the coming darkness, though

I am unable to act on them myself." He let out a long, pained cough. "Any medicine that could dull the pain would prevent my visions. I can, however, give you all reason to hope."

"The Shadow Glade faces destruction," Nareena said, resting her head in her hands. "If it falls, the enemy wins. As things stand, I fail to see how there is any reason for hope whatsoever."

"Your people were deceived," Eilith replied. "You were led to believe the Glade is the last outpost of the fairies, but it is no such thing. There are pockets of resistance all over the world."

"Even if that's true, how do we find them?" I blurted out, feeling another rush of embarrassment for speaking before the Queen.

"That I cannot tell you," Eilith said as he took a sharp breath, "but you will find a way. Whatever happens, Queen, you must protect the human children, as well as your siblings, for I sense they will have a role in deciding what happens..." He trailed off then, and with a last shuddering breath Eilith closed his eyes.

We waited for him to wake up, but I wasn't sure I could even see him breathing anymore. "I...I can't do this," I said after a few moments of stunned silence. "This isn't my war. I've not even finished school yet! You've obviously confused me for someone else. I want to go back to my parents."

"Clint, we do not ask this happily," Naarin said, placing his hand gently on my shoulder. "But if the enemy hasn't killed your parents already, it won't be long before they do. I cannot promise what will come next, but I *can* promise we'll do whatever it takes to—" His speech was cut short by a loud bang from somewhere outside the chamber. "What in *Matha'ra*'s name was that?"

"My lord," said a fairy guard as he rushed into the chamber, stopping when he realized he was in his Queen's presence. "My apologies, your highness, but the barrier is weakening rapidly; the enemy will breach the city walls very soon."

"What shall we do, sister?" Naarin asked, staring at Nareena intently. "I fear the time for just sitting around talking has long passed."

"I must agree," Nareena said, looking pensive for a moment. "Naarin, you and Arcturus have my full blessing to do whatever it takes to defend this city, but I'm telling you right now: if it comes down to saving your own lives or defending the city, you are to escape to our safe haven immediately."

"We're coming with you," Crystal said to the Queen as the fairies began to move. "We aren't trained to fight; our place isn't on a battlefield." She sounded nervous, and I didn't blame her.

"You're safer here if something goes wrong," Niana said firmly. "My sister will need to move quickly to get the civilians out of the city, which will mean flying." She walked over to me then, kissing me gently on the cheek and making me blush. "I promise we'll meet again, Clint; my brother knows I'll kill him if anything happens to you." She smiled at me before walking back over to her sister. "Good luck."

Before anyone could say another word the two had vanished, as if they'd just blinked out of existence in front of our very eyes.

"So…what do we do now?" Mickey asked, looking confused.

"You three stay with me," Naarin replied, nodding. "If you're going to be fighting alongside us, I think it's time we found you some armor." He looked at me, smiling slightly. "And some weapons."

Chapter 4

"What exactly are we supposed to do?" Mickey asked as Naarin led us to the armory, where several soldiers were taking up their weapons and armor. "I can't fight! The closest thing I've done is play computer games, and I'm not great at those either."

"Just stick next to me," Naarin said, handing us a sword and shield each. "I can't guarantee you'll be completely safe by my side, but you'll stand more chance than if you go off and try to do this yourselves."

At that moment, Nightshade and Nikkela entered the room. The healer had a bow over one shoulder and a quiver full of black-feathered arrows over the other.

"What are you two doing here?" Naarin asked, frowning. "I assumed you'd gone with my sister."

"I intended to," Nightshade replied, sounding a little irritated, "but she told me she thought you'd need my assistance more than she does."

"You're also going to need a healer more than she does," Nikkela said with a sigh. "Besides, you always seem to forget I'm one of the best archers in the Shadow Glade."

"Fine," Naarin said. "I guess the more weapons available to me, the better. Do we know what the situation's like out there?"

"The barrier is mere moments from falling," Nightshade replied. "Luckily for us, the sentinels are slowing the enemy's progress, but their numbers are few and they won't be able to hold them for long."

"Spread the forces out," Arcturus commanded as he walked into the room. "We don't number enough for a pitched battle, but if we fight them street-by-street we may stand a chance. Nightshade can take the right side of the city, Naarin, you defend the left. I'll defend the central route. If we spread a mix of weapons among each group, we'll be less likely to be overwhelmed."

"We'd better take up our positions then," Naarin said. "I'd like to give one last speech before the arrows start flying."

As we stepped out of the royal tower and into the central square there was a definite sense of tension in the air. As I walked, I caught the occasional glimpse of a Fairy soldier, hanging out in the alleys between buildings or peering out the windows of nearby houses. Some wore the long green cloaks of the sentinels, some were dressed like the city guards, and others were garbed as if they'd been interrupted during their work and had consequently just grabbed the nearest tool as a makeshift weapon.

Naarin took a moment to look around as Nightshade

and Arcturus took up their positions at the bottom of the steps.

"I don't need to remind you all what's at stake here," Naarin said loudly, addressing the people. "We have retreated long enough, so we need to make a stand here, now, or our enemy may never be stopped." There was a cheer that was low but just about audible. "I will not, however, ask you to take the ultimate risk; if we sound the retreat, you are to fall back to the tunnels immediately, and don't stop until you reach the safe havens at the other end. Good luck, and may Matha'ra be with us all."

"Good luck, Prince," Arcturus called after us as we headed away from the steps and down one of the side streets. I turned back and smiled, though it was rather half-hearted.

Eventually, we found our way to a spot where, along with a sizable group of archers, Nikkela was waiting. She flashed a smile in our direction.

"Clint, I'm scared," Crystal said suddenly, her sword arm shaking visibly. "I…I've never hurt anyone before."

"You'll be safe with us," Nikkela said, giving Crystal's shoulder a gentle squeeze to try and reassure her. "I'll do my best to stop them from reaching you."

Before Crystal could respond there was a bright burst of light above us as the barrier finally gave way, closely followed by a loud, inhuman shriek that seemed to ring out around the entire city.

"They're here, everyone, prepare to fire!" Nikkela said, nocking an arrow to her bow as she watched the streets in front of them for any signs of attack.

"Remember, some of them are resistant to magic," Naarin warned, drawing his own sword.

My two friends and I were the last to raise our weapons—making me feel slightly embarrassed at our slow reactions—but at first nothing seemed to happen, leading even Naarin to appear confused. Then, slowly, shadows began spreading across the ground as fallen fairies and Fenrir landed among the streets, some alighting on roofs and aiming their bows at the defenders.

"For every inch they take, make them pay with their blood!" Naarin shouted, loud enough for all the surrounding fairies to hear him, as the archers began loosing arrows.

"Stick with me," Nikkela said to us as one of her arrows felled a rogue fairy who'd either been brave or foolish enough to land in the middle of the street opposite us. "I wouldn't trust our princely friend to be able to focus on you in the middle of a battle."

"Something's wrong," Mickey said as one of the archers fell down in front of them, a javelin having gone right through his neck. "Am I the only one thinking they aren't making much effort to attack us here? It's almost like—"

"I was starting to think they're trying to distract us," Nikkela said, gritting her teeth. "Naarin, we're not the target. Where would…" She trailed off as she looked around the square, the realization hitting her and Naarin simultaneously. "The tunnels, they're trying to cut off our escape route! That way they can surround us and pick us off one by one."

"Nikkela, get to Nightshade," Naarin ordered, narrowly dodging another javelin. "Tell him to bring his troops toward the palace—I guess we've got a good old-fashioned last stand on our hands."

As Nikkela took off with a small spring they turned back toward the central square, only to find their way blocked by a Fenrir and a gang of rogue fairies. "I guess you guys will get a chance to fight after all," Naarin said to me, letting out a nervous laugh. "Leave the Fenrir to me; you're not experienced enough to fight him."

"I'm not going to argue with you there," I said as we turned our weapons upon the other fairies.

Whereas our allies seemed to fight gracefully—some of them appearing to almost dance between opponents—the fallen fairies were far more brutal; armed with short knives, they tried to hack at their opponents.

We carried on fighting, and even as the gang of enemies was slowly thinning, a grunt from behind us caught my attention. Naarin had been knocked to the ground and the Fenrir was looming over him, one fearsome-looking claw rising high, ready to strike. I made a move toward him, but Naarin shook his head as he sat up.

"Get out of here!" he shouted, raising his sword with a wince. "I'll be fine, Arcturus needs—" His speech was cut short by a gurgle escaping from the Fenrir's lips, and a moment later it collapsed, revealing a shaking Crystal standing in its place, her blood-slicked sword threatening to slip from her grasp. Naarin jumped to his feet, helping to steady her while also killing the fallen fairy who'd been about to attack Crystal from behind. "Are you okay, Crystal?" he asked, looking down at her still shaking form.

"I...I'll be fine," Crystal said, stepping away from Naarin and trying to smile. "We need to hurry up."

"Not gonna argue with you there," Naarin said as the troops around them dispatched what was left of the obstacle in front of them before running toward the square. As they reached it, they were confronted with the sight of Arcturus squaring off with a huge Fenrir who, even from a quick glance, I could tell was the creature from the clearing earlier.

"Spread out!" Naarin shouted, as much to Nightshade's forces appearing on the other side of the square as to his own. "Don't let that creature's buddies interfere in this fight!"

"Watch out!" I shouted as Mickey ducked under the swing of a fairy blade, one of Nikkela's superbly-shot arrows felling the warrior before it could bring the sword back around for another swing. "For every enemy we kill, there seem to be five more, Naarin," I said, looking around frantically at the numerous bodies on both sides. "I hate to sound defeatist but we need to put our exit plan into action."

"Exactly as I was thinking, Clint," Naarin said with a grimace. "Arcturus, sound the retreat!" he called out. "My sister was right; this city isn't worth us losing our lives over."

"That's the wisest thing you've said in years," Arcturus said with a chuckle as he ducked a swipe from one of the claws of his opponent, then decapitated his foe with one deft flick of his sword. "Defenders of the Glade, retreat! We will live to fight another day."

"Arcturus, look out!" Crystal shouted, not quite loud enough for him to hear her above the noise, although Mickey and I immediately spotted what she'd seen.

A fallen fairy had taken off unseen and was now aiming a javelin at the General's back. The warning had come too late, and even as Arcturus heard a yell from the other side of the square the javelin hit him straight through his back, making him stagger.

On the other side of the street Nightshade moved quicker than I thought possible given his bulk, launching himself into the air on a pair of thin but formidable-looking wings, his sword drawn and gripped tightly in his hand.

While the assailant saw Nightshade coming, his reflexes were just too slow, and his lifeless body crashed to the floor as Nightshade made a beeline for Arcturus. Mickey, Crystal, Naarin, and I reached his side a moment later.

"I'll get Nikkela," Naarin said, helping Arcturus stand up. "We can fix this."

"No," Arcturus said, pushing his helping hand away. "It's already too late for me. Besides, you made me a promise that when the time came, you'd make sure she didn't have to see me like this. I'll take as many of them with me as I can, but you need to take this and go," he added, handing over a sword almost as ornate as Nightshade's own weapon.

"I…I can't," Naarin said, the shock clear in his voice.

"This is the badge of office for the Army of the Glade, I have no right to—"

"You have every right to it," Arcturus said, cutting off his protest. "Nightshade has no interest in leading the army, and these men would follow you to the gates of the underworld itself if you asked them to. Now, go! Don't let me die in vain."

"I…" Naarin paused for a moment, undecided, before the screech of more Fenrir approaching made his mind up for him. "Fairies of the Glade, you know where to go! Fall back! We'll meet at the safe haven, our Queen awaits us there." He turned to me and the others then. "Follow me and Nightshade; we'll keep you safe."

I glanced at Arcturus sadly before focusing back on Nightshade and Naarin.

Nightshade seemed filled with a rage that made the enemy wary to approach as we made a beeline for the palace, the few who attempted to approach him being felled with a vicious swipe of his blade.

Naarin led us to the side of the tower, where we found a door no more visible than the one in the tree trunk. Naarin opened it to shoo us through, before pausing for just a moment to look back at the sight of the carnage we were leaving behind.

"Are you okay?" I asked him as I ducked through the doorway. The image of Arcturus lying on the ground was still foremost in my mind.

"Hmm? Yeah," Naarin said after a moment, closing the door behind us. "Let's not dally here; we face a long trek ahead of us."

There were only a handful of scattered lanterns in the tunnel, making it difficult to judge how far we'd traveled and how far we still had to travel, but I was glad of Mickey's help in supporting Crystal, who was seemingly suffering a fresh wave of shock from what she'd just witnessed—and what she'd just done. I didn't blame her.

Suddenly, I caught sight of a pool of light in the tunnel ahead, and rounding a corner, we found Nikkela sitting on the floor, her wings folded close to her body, her arms hiding her face that was resting on her knees. Without a word Naarin ran over to her, draping his cloak around her shoulders and holding her close as Nightshade dropped to the floor.

"Make yourself comfortable," Nightshade said with a sigh. "We all need to take a breather before we continue."

"I don't understand," Mickey said, trying to avoid looking at the two fairies sitting together on the ground. "Nikkela—"

"Is in love with the Prince?" Nightshade finished with a chuckle. "Their love is the worst kept secret in the whole of the Glade."

"I meant what Arcturus said," Mickey continued, raising his eyebrows. "Is there nothing Nikkela could have done?"

"It's not whether she could have healed him," Nightshade replied, frowning, "it's…well, Arcturus was Nikkela's grandfather, and when her father died in front of her and her mother vanished, Arcturus made us all promise she'd never have to see him meet his death." He looked across at Crystal, who was in tears herself, and reaching into his cloak he handed her a strange biscuit-like object. "Eat this, Crystal," he said. "I'd forgotten you wouldn't have killed before; this will at least help you feel a little calmer."

"Thank…thank you," Crystal stuttered, biting into the biscuit. As she looked up, she froze. "Guys, we have company."

We all looked up, finding ourselves suddenly surrounded by black-robed figures, each one holding a bow with a wickedly sharp arrow nocked to it. All of us drew our weapons in unison—even Nikkela, who drew a short dagger she had at her belt.

"Drop your weapons, intruders," came a voice from somewhere in the shadows.

"Not till your men lower theirs," Naarin replied, without missing a beat. "We're merely resting here; you threaten us for no reason."

"I must insist," the voice replied. "Lower your weapons. I will not warn you again."

"And if we don't?" Nightshade called out.

"Believe me, you don't want to know the answer to that question," came the reply, as a female fairy even taller than Nightshade stepped out from the shadows. She was dressed in a long dark cloak, the hood hiding her hair and a scarf pulled over the lower half of her face, revealing only a pair of golden eyes that stared intently at the group in front of her. She pulled back her hood to reveal long, spiky red hair.

"You! No, you can't be here," Nikkela gasped, backing away from the fairy.

"Who is it?" I asked, noting the surprise on Nightshade and Naarin's faces as well.

"Her name is Desha'yi," Naarin replied, a note of disbelief in his voice. "She's Nikkela's mother."

Chapter 5

"Where have you been?" Nikkela shouted furiously. "I've needed you all my life and you haven't given a damn about me! And you turn up *now*? Grandfather would be ashamed of you!"

"You think I *wanted* to leave you alone?" Desha'yi replied, her voice shaking. "I had no choice; your life would have been at risk if I'd stayed!"

"I know this reunion is not...ideal," Naarin said, stepping between the two of them as he sensed Nikkela's rage increasing, "but our kind has enough enemies already without us fighting each other. I'm sure your mother will explain everything to you soon, Nikkela, but just for now, can you please calm down?"

Nikkela sighed, nodding as she stepped back slightly.

"Tell your men to lower their weapons, Desha'yi—we are no threat to them."

"What on earth are you doing down here?" Desha'yi said as she nodded at her followers, and they lowered their weapons. "I'd assumed these tunnels were long forgotten by those on the surface, so what is my daughter, a Prince, and the royal guard doing down here? Not to mention the humans!"

"You've been out of the Glade society for far too long," Naarin replied. "The Glade has fallen; we were fleeing for the Silver Haven when our paths crossed. As for the humans, they are among the Chosen; they would be dead already but for my orders to intervene before the enemy reached them."

"This is grave news indeed," Desha'yi said as the shock spread across her face. "What of my father? Has he…" She trailed off as she saw tears spring into Nikkela's eyes at the mention of Arcturus. "What happened to him?"

"He was attacked by a coward," Naarin replied, looking down at his feet. "It didn't kill him outright, but the last I saw of him he was fighting to take as many of our foes with him as he could." He paused for a moment to allow the news to sink in. "Desha'yi, we need every fairy's help we can get—come with us, I'm sure my sister would welcome you."

"I have no place in your family's court," Desha'yi replied. "Your mother made that abundantly clear to me long before my exile."

"That was my mother," Naarin replied, "she and my sister are not the same person. Besides, you owe your daughter an explanation."

"I'll take you along these tunnels and back to our sanctuary," Desha'yi said, putting a hand up to stop the protest her comment was threatening to unleash. "You all look like you could do with a rest, besides which, if I and my kin are to come with you there are some things we need to gather first."

"As you wish," Naarin replied, before Nikkela could say anything, "lead the way."

The tunnels got wider and more brightly lit as Desha'yi and the others led us onward, and soon we arrived in a large cavern, which had been adapted into some form of underground camp. Hammocks and beds were littered around the cavern, female fairies and small children among those who greeted us cautiously. I watched Nightshade, Mickey, Crystal, and Nikkela go off to accept food from the cavern-dwellers, noticing the healer avoiding her mother as subtly as she could. Naarin, on the other hand, sat down on a low bunk bed on one side of the cavern, looking unfazed as I sat opposite him.

"Prince…Naarin, can I ask you a question?"

"Of course, you can," he replied, giving me a weak smile. "I'm sorry, this must all be so hectic for you," he added, sighing. "You haven't had much chance to adjust to what living among fairies is like, have you?"

I shrugged. "What happened to Nikkela's father? I don't feel comfortable asking Nikkela herself, and I'm definitely not walking up to someone I've only just stopped being threatened by for information."

"Good point," Naarin replied with a wry laugh. "Well, it happened back before the threat escalated, when fairies could still walk within the forest without any difficulties. Nikkela's parents took her out for a picnic one day in the warm summer sunshine, believing it would be safe, but it wasn't: they were attacked by a Nightstalker. No one's quite sure what happened, but when the sentinels found them hours later her father was dead, still hugging her unconscious form to his chest in an attempt to protect her. Her mother was nowhere to be seen, and—until just now—no one had seen her since."

"I had my reasons," Desha'yi said as she approached, clearly having been listening in. "Do not assume to judge me when you weren't there." Her tone was part defensive, part angry.

"I may not have been there when she was hurt," Naarin said, standing up to face Desha'yi as he clearly tried to contain his anger, "but I was by her bedside every night as she recovered. Where were you? Every night she woke up from a nightmare, screaming out for her mother who never arrived. Do you know she still carries the scar on her stomach from that day?"

"I...I didn't know," Desha'yi said, hanging her head in shame. "I *am* sorry, Naarin. Really. I took no pleasure in walking away from my daughter."

"I'm not the one you should be apologizing to," Naarin said with a sigh. "I can't tell you what you should say or what Nikkela needs to hear, but you could do worse than saying you're sorry and that you love her." He offered the woman a smile as she headed off in the direction of her daughter, then sat back down on the bed. "I expect none of your fairy tales told you about this side of our lives."

"Let's just say love wasn't the main theme in most of the stories my parents gave me to read," I said, looking down at the floor for a moment as I thought of my family.

"I'm sorry if this is a little…personal…but are you in love with Nikkela?"

Naarin shook his head. "It's not as simple as that—not among my kin, anyway," he replied. "We don't simply fall in love at the drop of a hat; when we bond, we bond for life. For all my teasing of her, my sister remains alone because she doesn't feel she can risk the possibility of falling in love with the wrong person. I and Nikkela bonded because I was there by her side when no one else was." He sighed as he looked up at the noisy room, where the others were clearing up in the center. His eyes particularly alighted upon Crystal, who was speaking to a young female fairy while helping her pack all the food they could find into a set of bags. "I hadn't realized you children would take all of this in your stride."

"Well, I guess we feel like we have friends here," I replied. "I know, that sounds ridiculous considering we'd never met any of you before all this started happening, but it's true." I shrugged.

"Believe me, I've heard stranger things in my life," Naarin said with a laugh. "Why don't you mingle for a bit? I'd like a few moments alone before we set out once again."

"Sure," I said as I stood up, sensing something was wrong but being unwilling to intrude upon his personal thoughts. I found my way over to where Nikkela and Mickey were helping a pair of young fairy children pack up their toys. "Do we know what this place is called?" I asked suddenly, wanting to avoid adding to the awkward silence that seemed to be hovering between the two of them.

"The Hall of the Phoenix," Nikkela replied, turning slightly and giving me what appeared to be a rather forced smile. "None of these fairies seem to know why it's called that, though; I get the feeling this place existed long before they came here." As she turned around, she caught sight of Crystal, deep in conversation with her companion. "It seems Crystal has made a new friend," she commented.

"Has she?" I asked, trying to avoid looking in their direction. "I thought she was just lending a hand with the evacuation..."

"Clint Jones, are you jealous?" Mickey asked, raising an eyebrow. "I know you mean a lot to Crystal, but you really aren't her type." He smiled before adding, "No offence."

"What do you mean?" I asked, especially when I noticed Nikkela stifling a giggle. "I've missed something, haven't I?"

"Let's just say there's a reason her and Nara are getting on like a house on fire," Nikkela said, trying to look apologetic. "Besides, in my opinion, you and Niana make quite the cute couple."

"Me and..." I paused, blushing bright red. "I don't know what you're talking about."

"Oh, come on, Clint," Mickey replied. "If a fairy who's known you five minutes can tell you're attracted to someone, there's probably something in it—never mind the fact I've seen chilli less red than you are right now."

"We're ready to move out!" Desha'yi called out before I could make any further statements. "Soldiers at the edge of the travelling party! The sick, the elderly, and children at the center! Hopefully this trip won't take too long. And no one gets left behind," she added, turning to meet the stare she was getting from Nikkela. "I've made that mistake enough times in my life."

I was glad to have Desha'yi leading us along the tunnel, as otherwise I'd have been completely lost—there was no indication as to which direction we were going in, and therefore I had no idea whether we were traveling the right way or not. I was walking at the front with Nightshade, Naarin was somewhere further back, and Mickey was trying to locate Crystal, as we hadn't seen her since the group had formed at the start of the journey.

I looked along the walls of the tunnel, which were lit with the same lights as the first fairy tunnel I'd seen, although these ones were brighter and spaced out more regularly along the walls. Occasionally we passed an alcove that had a statue of a strange, fantastical-looking creature carved into the rock wall, with strange writing beneath that was presumably intended to identify the creature but which I found completely indecipherable.

Suddenly—just as I noticed the heavy clunk of Nightshade's armored feet stomping along beside me—I felt a tap on my shoulder, and I turned to find Crystal.

"I think I owe you an explanation and an apology," she said quietly, looking at the ground rather than making eye contact with me.

"How long have you known?" I asked.

"That I'm a lesbian?" Crystal asked, laughing slightly.

"Seriously, Clint, you don't need to feel shy—I'm the one who mucked up."

"I'm not angry, I have no reason to be angry," I said. "Really, don't apologize. I want you to be happy, I just…I guess I'm surprised it took me this long to figure it out."

"Not many people know," Crystal admitted. "Mickey only does because he caught me having my first kiss. Remember Becky Cole?"

"Becky?" I asked, raising an eyebrow. "Seriously, she was your first kiss? I thought you hated each other?"

"We do," Crystal replied, laughing. "Pretty much the only thing I *don't* regret about that kiss is the fact it made me realize who I really am. I don't broadcast it because my family…well, I'm not saying they hate gay people, but my mum is a little…"

"Traditional?"

"Exactly," Crystal said, sighing. "If we get out of this alive and my parents are still around, I think it's time I was finally honest with them. I mean…I might have someone to bring home to meet them."

"What's her name?" I asked, laughing at her embarrassment. "I think the whole cavern saw who you were being chummy with, Crystal."

"You're worse than the cool clique when it comes to gossip," Crystal said, rolling her eyes. "There's nothing happening there—yet. But since you insist on being nosey, her name is Nara. I don't even know if she likes me; apparently she just finds me more interesting than most of the other people she's crossed paths with."

"Stop!" Naarin shouted before I could utter another word.

For a moment I was confused as to what had caused the sudden halt, but when I looked up, I saw a massive gate just a matter of meters in front of us. Two fairies were situated at the top of the wall, leaning on long spears, though they didn't appear to have noticed our approach.

"We seek entry to the Silver Haven!" Naarin shouted up.

"And why should we…" one of the guards started saying, before seeing Naarin. Then, nodding, he turned toward the gate. "Open the doors, our Prince has returned!"

As the gates opened and we began to step inside, Mickey, Crystal, and I were given a bit of a shock. Rather than another underground cavern we'd been expecting to see, above us there was a cloudy sky, the towering walls of a fortress surrounding us on all sides.

"I should have told you the Silver Haven is an old human castle," Naarin said, taking in our expressions. "It's surprising what happens when humans lose interest in their history."

"I can't even tell where this is," Mickey said, looking up at the walls. "My history teacher would give me an F for not spotting this immediately."

"Is everyone here?" I asked, looking around, only to be caught off guard when Niana appeared in front of me and threw her arms around my shoulders. I laughed, embarrassed, uncertain if I should withdraw from the hug or not, to the evident amusement of my friends and the Prince.

"When you didn't arrive, I threatened to come look for you myself," she said, kissing me lightly and laughing at my embarrassment. "No offence, brother," she added, casting her gaze toward Naarin, "but you're not getting a kiss off me; I knew you'd get back here in one piece."

"Thanks, sis," Naarin said with a wry chuckle. "Where's our sister? I have some interesting news to deliver to her."

"She's taken up residence in the old mess hall," Niana replied, finally letting go of me. "I guess I'll see to our new arrivals then." With that she led Nikkela and the others away, flashing one last smile in my direction.

"Don't worry, Clint," Naarin said, smiling at me. "There are far worse people my sister could show an interest in, most of whom are other fairies."

We picked our way through the ruined corridors until we found our destination: a solid-looking door that was standing ajar, and that was being guarded by two weary-looking figures leaning on short spears. When they saw us, they stepped aside, letting us into a room that had been furnished with only a low table and a handful of chairs, the largest of which seated the Queen, who looked even weaker than she had when I'd first met her. Her adviser knelt down beside her, and at the sound of our approach she looked up, smiling. She made no move to get out of her seat.

"It is a great relief to see you alive," she said. "I was concerned after I heard about Arcturus."

"My Queen, what's happened?" Nightshade asked, walking over to her. "Should I get the healer?"

"I will be...better soon," Nareena said, waving his concern away. "Maintaining the barrier while it was under attack was far more of a strain than I'd remembered; I simply need time to recover."

"What you *need* is help, sister," Naarin said. "Luckily I may have found some. I'm...I'm not sure you'll like it, though," he added, stepping aside to reveal Desha'yi standing behind him, waiting cautiously.

"Desha'yi, is that really you?" Nareena asked, squinting at her. "Great Gaia, I thought I'd never see you again!"

"My apologies, Queen," Desha'yi said, curtsying. "I hadn't realised your mother no longer ruled; I thought I would be unwelcome here."

"You were more of a mother to me than my own ever was," Nareena said, smiling. "You are always welcome here." She indicated the seats opposite her before asking, "I'm guessing the good news extends beyond simply discovering our lost friends?"

"I believe I know where to find more allies," Desha'yi said as she sat down in one of the chairs. "In my home...where I was before Naarin brought me here...we had a fairy who claimed to be half-Cornish Pixie. According to her, there are still many Pixies living in Cornwall—if you know where to find them."

"This is risky," Naarin said, shaking his head. "I don't

like it. We only have one fairy's word for it, and even if it's true, Pixies aren't exactly renowned for being friendly to other species."

"If Desha'yi trusts this half-Pixie then so do I," Nareena replied. "Besides, we cannot remain in this Haven for long, not without risking our enemy following us here—we could lose this safe place permanently. The only problem is, how do we get there? We cannot move everyone in this Haven to Cornwall that easily."

"We may have a solution for that," Nightshade said suddenly, his gaze suddenly focused in the direction of the door. "I believe we have company."

We turned to find Crystal and Nara standing there, along with another creature who looked very different to the other fairies in the room. It was a woman, but she was far more delicate in appearance than even the fairy Queen, with wings more like a dragonfly's. Bright green hair hung over her face, half-hiding her thin lips and a pair of ruby red eyes.

"My apologies, Your Majesty," Nara said, looking at us sheepishly. "I didn't wish to intrude, but she insisted on speaking to you urgently."

"Who is she?" Naarin asked, looking between Nara and the newcomer.

"My name is Finarae," the woman answered. "I come from Nara's people, and we have much to discuss. My lady may have found a way to destroy the enemy."

Chapter 6

"The guards gave us no indication of her approach," Nightshade said, reaching for his sword. "She could be anyone, your highness. Do you wish me to remove her from the Haven?"

"I can vouch for her," Nara said before the pixie could respond. "And if that's not enough for you, I would hope that Desha'yi at least trusts me."

"Calm yourself, old friend," Nareena said, resting a hand on her guard's arm. "I can tell she's genuine: she has no hostile intentions toward us, I'm sure."

Nightshade hesitated, though he eventually returned his sword to its sheath.

"How can you be so certain?" I asked the Queen, trying not to sound as suspicious as I felt.

"My sister has powers your kind would probably call...telepathy, I suppose," Naarin replied, clearly choosing his words carefully. "It is difficult—if not impossible—to hide your inner thoughts from her. Believe me, that got me in considerable trouble when we were younger." He grinned at me, then stood up as Nara, Crystal, and Finarae approached. "Take a seat; you look tired," he said to Finarae.

"I thank you," the Pixie said, sitting down in a chair next to me.

Sitting at such close quarters, I could see she wasn't quite as young and healthy as I'd initially assumed; while she was certainly a younger woman, her face was covered in what appeared to be wrinkles, and she had a hook-shaped scar on one cheek. Emerging from her cloak, one of her arms was encased in an armored gauntlet, but where her other arm should've been there was little more than a stump. When I realized she'd noticed me looking I felt embarrassed, though she seemed to be amused by the attention rather than annoyed, which turned my embarrassment to relief.

"You didn't think the enemy only exists where you live, did you?"

I shook my head, unable to think of anything to say.

"Do you require any refreshment?" Nareena asked. "I can't promise you a feast in the current circumstances, but I'm sure we can offer you some kind of food or drink."

"I had a large meal before I left," Finarae replied, "but thank you for asking. Anyway, I believe we have more urgent matters to discuss."

"You mentioned that your mistress had found something," Naarin said, pre-empting his sister. "What exactly were you talking about?"

"Our scouts have been patrolling the Cornish cities and towns for months now," Finarae replied, "more for the protection of humans than our own kind. Up until three days ago we'd found nothing of interest, but then one of our patrols came across a wounded fallen fairy. He claimed to have been escaping from a large gathering of our enemy, even promising to take us there so we could see it for ourselves and decide what action to take."

"I hate to ruin the good mood," Nikkela interrupted, suddenly appearing behind Naarin to the surprise of everyone in the room, "but assuming what she says is true, why did the Pixies have to find us? There's something she's yet to tell us."

"We have already made an attempt to scout out the area," the Pixie replied, visibly annoyed by the interruption. "The force there is larger than any we have previously been confronted with—it includes Fenrir, Nightstalkers, and many other creatures we've never laid eyes on before. We believe a direct confrontation is demanded, but we simply do not have the forces to take it on alone."

"While this is a cause I'm sympathetic toward," Nareena said after a short pause, "we don't have many soldiers to offer you; if you're looking for an army to fight a war for you, I'm afraid you'll have to look elsewhere." There was regret in her voice, but not much.

"We are not alone in this battle," Finarae said. "There are others of my kin out there in the country, finding whatever help wherever they can. I am partly here to request help in recruiting some fairies who are, let's say, a little…difficult…to reach."

"I will have to discuss this with my brother," Nareena said, cutting off Naarin's attempt at protestation before he could utter a single word. "They are his soldiers, so I cannot dispatch them on a mission without first ensuring he is comfortable doing so."

As Finarae bowed and stood up, the Queen turned to face me. "I mean no offence to you or your friends, Clint, but this is a matter we must discuss alone. Naarin will come and find you once we've decided on our next move."

As everyone but Naarin, Nareena, and Nightshade left the chamber, we made our way back to the central courtyard, and as the others looked for food I walked over to where Nikkela was treating one of the sentinel's wounds. There was little more than a grunt of acknowledgement from the soldier, while Nikkela pretended she hadn't noticed me. This pretense lasted only for a few seconds.

"I should thank you," Nikkela said, finishing off the bandage she was wrapping. "You are, at least in part, responsible for my mother and I finding each other again."

"I did nothing," I said, sitting down as the soldier got up and walked away. "It was Naarin who lectured her about speaking to you; I just sat there and listened to their argument. I haven't ever done anything impressive in my entire life," I added, shrugging, "I don't know why your people think I could be even remotely special."

"That is precisely why you and your friends are what we need," Nikkela said, sitting next to me. "You humans think of heroism as involving spectacular acts of violence or people fighting purely for their own selfish ends. That is *not* heroic, and it's certainly not courageous. Real heroes care about doing the right thing, however big a risk it means taking. They care about other people ahead of themselves." She looked at me, clearly upset though she was trying to smile. "I may never have met her, but if I could find a way to bring your own mother back, I would. We all would."

"I know," I replied, looking at the floor. "I suspect Naarin would lead a party himself to at least discover what her ultimate fate was, but I just can't ask him to do that. He has more than enough to worry about as things are, and I should be helping you, not thinking of myself."

"If more humans were like you, Clint, this world would be a much happier place," Nikkela said, gently putting an arm around me and hugging me briefly. "Do you want to know what my mother said to me?"

"Shouldn't you tell Naarin first?" I asked, immediately worrying that I'd sounded like I'd snapped at her. "Not that I'm not interested, but I know you and Naarin are close."

"You're right," she replied, "but there's part of this you should know first. Have you ever seen this symbol before?" She pulled a medallion out of her cloak, and I leaned forward to get a closer look. It bore a picture of a wolf, on whose back was perched a huge eagle.

"My mum had a similar picture by her bed," I replied, studying it. "I only saw it a handful of times because she rarely let me in her room. What are you trying to tell me?"

"It's my family crest, Clint," Nikkela replied. "I'm not sure how this came about, but your mother is Desha'yi's sister, which makes us—"

"Cousins!" I said, shocked. "But...how? Is your mother sure?"

Nikkela nodded. "As it turns out, the story I was told of what happened the day my father died was only partially true," she replied. "The picnic was merely the cover my parents used to flee the Shadow Glade; they were going to warn your parents that your mother's life may be in danger from the forces of darkness. Unfortunately, said forces found them before we could flee, leaving my mother with an impossible choice: as they knew she'd survived the attack, whether she came back for me or carried on to your mother, either way she was going to put someone she cared about in mortal danger. Thus, she made the difficult decision to go underground and wait until she felt the time was right to return to the outside world."

"So, them targeting me was no accident, then?" I asked, still trying to get my head around this new revelation.

"None of you were targeted accidentally," Nikkela replied. "My mother believes the Watchers have—either knowingly or unknowingly—been guarding half-fairy children the entire time, partly because you're the greatest threat to our enemy's plan to crush any fairies who won't bow to them."

"Mickey and Crystal need to know," I said after a few moments. "If their families are in any kind of danger, they deserve the chance to at least warn them...perhaps there's some kind of precaution they can take."

"I agree, Clint," Nikkela said, "but I get the feeling that may have to wait." She nodded at where Naarin and the Queen had entered the central courtyard, Nightshade close behind them.

The bodyguard let out a loud cough to get everyone's attention, and all fell silent.

"My brother and I have a plan," Nareena said to the expectant faces now gathered around her. "This Haven is safe enough—at least for the moment—for the wounded, the elderly, the young, and any who wish to stay here. Nightshade and I will remain with you in order to help you feel safe. Meanwhile, Naarin, Finarae, Nara, our human friends, and some of our soldiers have an important mission to undertake elsewhere in these islands. If they succeed, we'll find new allies and be able to take one great step closer to avenging our fallen friends. Those who are going had best gather what you need quickly; you'll be leaving soon."

"You'll need me," Nikkela said, walking over to Naarin as the Queen departed the courtyard again. "Even if we can travel there safely, we may well have to offer aid to our new friends. Plus, as I showed in the Glade, if the need arises I'm more than capable of fighting."

"Me too," Niana said, appearing behind me and playfully ruffling my hair, then sighing when she saw the disapproving look her brother gave her. "I've spent too long doing nothing, brother; I need to get out there, to feel like I'm at least doing *something* to help our cause."

"Great Gaia, is there any point in me arguing?" Naarin asked, letting out a wry laugh. "Something tells me you'll come whether I like it or not, and I suppose I'd rather have you with us where I can keep a friendly eye on you."

"Are you at least going to tell us where we're going?" Nikkela asked, moving next to Naarin and taking his hand. "You seem unusually secretive. What exactly are we walking into?"

"We're going to Ireland," Naarin replied. "We're going to try and find the Sidhe."

"Are you serious?" Niana asked, her mouth agape.

"What's so exciting?" Mickey asked as he, Crystal, and Nara walked up. "What exactly are the Sidhe?"

"They're one of the oldest fairy races in recorded history," Nara replied. "If they're still alive, the side they choose in this war may be crucial."

Thankfully for my friends and I, we teleported to Ireland—negating the problem of us having no wings of our own—and in an instant our surroundings had changed from the huge fortress to rolling grassland. We were now surrounded by numerous low hills, on the tops of which there were several stone buildings dotted about. Although we sent scouts into the countryside to try and find some sign of the Sidhe, after three hours we'd found little sign of life beyond the occasional bird.

At Finarae's instruction we made camp; she told us that if the Sidhe *were* nearby, they'd come to us by themselves.

As darkness fell—our presence still seemingly having gone unnoticed—various occupants of the camp (with the exception of a small number of guards) slowly made their way to tents or blankets that were laid on the ground.

I, however, was finding it very difficult to sleep, and as I lay under my own blanket I stared at the fire in the center of camp.

Suddenly I heard a noise coming from behind me, and when I turned around, I found Niana crouched down in the grass.

"I'm glad to see I'm not the only one who can't sleep," she said, sitting down. "I guess I'm just not used to sleeping out in the open." She sighed. "I thought we'd have found something by now, and I don't like it; I can feel a growing sense of unease lying around out here."

"Me too," I said, reassured to learn someone else was concerned as well, and when I realised Niana was shivering, I asked, "Do...do you want to snuggle up under here? I mean... I don't want you to get cold as well as being exhausted."

"You're even cuter when you're embarrassed," Niana said with a laugh, getting under the blanket and, before I could say or do anything else, pulling me into a kiss, which caused me to blush. "What's wrong?" she asked, before the realization hit her. "You've never kissed a girl before, have you?"

"No," I replied. "I haven't. I know that probably spoils the moment."

"Not at all," she said with a sweet smile. "Better make sure this is memorable then." She put an arm around the back of my head, kissing me again, and once the initial shock had worn off, I happily reciprocated.

The kiss seemed to last for ages, and we only stopped when we were interrupted by a loud howl from somewhere nearby.

"What the hell was that?" I asked, pulling away from her slightly to look around. "There aren't any wolves around here, not unless my knowledge of British history is worse than I thought."

"It wasn't a wolf, Clint," said Niana, sitting up and looking over me toward the fire. "We have a problem."

I rolled over to find that the camp was suddenly filled with strange figures. Taller than Nightshade, they showed no visible sign of having wings, or any other recognizably fairy features. Some were riding large dragonflies while others were on foot, but all of them were heavily armed.

Standing near the fire was a female warrior in jade-colored armor, a long brown cape flowing from her back and a knife in her hand, held out to Crystal's throat, who she had locked in the tight grip of her arms. A quick glance revealed Nara's unconscious, but still alive, form lying nearby.

"Let her go!" I shouted, standing up and drawing the blade Naarin had given me, Niana doing the same with hers. "Who the hell are you?"

"Oh, I hadn't realised the people of England were so brave," the strange woman replied, cackling. "Boy, you are trespassing on Sidhe land, and if you don't give me a good reason for your intrusion on the Great Hunt, I will ensure this land runs red with your blood before the night is out!"

Chapter 7

"Like hell am I telling you anything while you threaten my friend!" I shouted, taking a step forward but feeling Niana's arm reaching out to stop me.

"I understand that you're upset, Clint," Niana whispered, "but let's be realistic here: she has us outnumbered, they're better armed…never mind the fact they were able to get into our camp completely unseen. Maybe aggression isn't the best option? You can't just start giving out orders." She let out a sigh of relief as I lowered my blade, before turning back to the mystery newcomer. "Where are the others?" she barked out. "If you've done anything—"

"You'll what?" the woman asked, raising an eyebrow. "You're in no position to threaten me, but—to reassure you—your companions are fast asleep, my soldiers have seen to that. For some reason only the four of you were awake to hear our approach. Now," she said, finally releasing Crystal, who quickly ran to Nara's side, "you still haven't explained what you're doing in the land of the Sidhe."

"Do you not know of the war the world is facing?" Niana asked. "We came here to ask you for aid; we didn't expect to be threatened."

"We Sidhe don't involve ourselves in the affairs of others," the woman replied, sounding unconcerned. "So, go home, deal with whatever enemy you think you have to face, and leave us out of your petty squabbles."

"And what do you think they'll do if they beat us?" Crystal yelled as the Sidhe turned away. "I don't know if they've reached Ireland already, but if they haven't it won't take long, and by that point there won't be any fairies to protect help you."

"You're a brave one, girl, I'll give you that," the woman said, turning to one of the nearby dragonfly riders for a moment, before turning around again. "So be it; you will be given the chance to state your case to my Queen. But only as my prisoners."

"Don't argue," Niana said, grasping my hand tightly to stop me from taking any further action. "It may be our only route into their city, and if we get ourselves killed trying to force our way in, we won't be doing anyone any favors."

We soon found ourselves being marched toward one of the large hills we'd seen in the distance, surrounded by guards while the dragonflies flew a short distance above us. The others had since been woken up: Naarin, Mickey, and

Finarae were chained together near me, with Niana at the front of the group. The woman who'd threatened Crystal was in front of us and Nara was on a makeshift stretcher being carried by two of the Sidhe guards, with Crystal walking next to her.

"I don't understand," Mickey said, trying to focus on what was ahead. "You said we were looking for fairies, but these creatures don't look like fairies at all."

"They *are* fairies," Finarae answered, "but they developed in a very different way to the fairies in the rest of the British Isles. In fact, what you see aren't the original Sidhe anyway; they are their descendants."

"The difference being what, exactly?" I asked. "Besides the fact that I don't see any wings on them."

"Oh, they have wings," Finarae replied, "but due to some genetic quirk they get folded close to their skin when not in use, so if they're wearing clothes the wings are invisible, unless you look closely." She sighed. "That's not the difference I'm referring to, however. Long ago, before your kind began to forget our existence, Sidhe were one of the fairy races who maintained a strong presence among the humans—there are even stories of one of the old Irish kings taking a Sidhe princess as his wife—but when the English came here they tried to take the fight to the Sidhe, an ambition which could never succeed against the magic of the Queen. However, the losses were sufficient that they withdrew to the fortresses hidden below the ground, and as they became steadily more isolationist, they cut themselves off even from other fairies: my kind were the last they maintained regular contact with. It had long been rumored that they'd since become hostile to almost any creature who crossed their path."

"But if they remain underground, what is this 'Great Hunt' they referred to?" I asked.

"I'll tell you later," Finarae said, suddenly looking nervous.

I looked up to see what had caused her discomfort; we'd reached the hill we'd been able to see in the near distance, but what I'd assumed to be a rocky outcrop was actually a large, rocky opening. On either side of this opening there stood two tall Sidhe, leaning on long pikes while holding towering shields in their other hands.

Before I could say anything else we were bundled through the entrance by the guards and plunged into pitch-black surroundings.

We eventually found ourselves thrown into cells somewhere below the level of the entrance; our soldiers were thrown in one cell, while I found myself in another, along with the rest of our party. Once the cell door was closed behind us Nikkela made her way over to the unconscious form of Nara, who was still lying on the stretcher. Crystal hovered anxiously nearby as she waited for news.

"She'll recover," Nikkela said as she reached into her pouch of medicine. "I suspect whoever attacked her wasn't attempting to seriously harm her, otherwise her condition would be far more serious. I don't understand why they attacked straight away instead of attempting to approach us peacefully, though."

"Because I hadn't considered the Great Hunt," Finarae said, grimacing. "Otherwise, I would have chosen a better location for us to set up camp."

"And a Great Hunt would be…?" Mickey asked scornfully.

"The Sidhe carry it out once a month," Finarae replied. "It used to be that they'd hunt an animal of their choice— even farm animals if it took their fancy—and then return without being seen by any humans. At least, the humans had better hope they didn't catch sight of the royal court."

"What do you mean?" I asked.

"It is said that if a human's path were to cross with that of the royal court, they would be made a seemingly irresistible offer," Finarae answered. "They would be offered a place among the Queen's courtiers, where they would have all the food they desired, live longer than any ordinary human, and be granted a place on every Great Hunt, but this offer came with a price: if the person attempted to escape, became separated from the Great Hunt, or was exiled by the Queen, they would age rapidly and die soon after. As I said, smart humans avoid the Hunt as if their lives depend upon it—because they do."

"That felt less like a hunt and more like a small army," Naarin said, rubbing his chin thoughtfully. "I'm guessing something happened to change them?"

"Like I said, after the invasion of Ireland they retreated," Finarae explained. "The last time the Pixies spoke to them a new Queen had been installed, one who believed non-Sidhe were attempting to corrupt her kin; she announced that she wouldn't allow anyone to threaten her culture. We tried to ask them to at least allow us to speak to them in the event of an emergency, but they flatly refused, saying the rest of the world was no longer their concern. I'm astonished, frankly, that they've even deemed us worthy of being considered for an audience. I must confess, I feared you may have refused to come on this trip at all, considering the risk."

"You'll have to excuse me if I don't feel entirely special," Mickey scoffed. "Quite frankly, right now I'm wondering why I'm here at all—with all due respect to Clint, I never asked to be taken on a hunt for fairies around the British Isles; he was the one whose family was threatened, not me."

"That's only partly true," Nikkela said with a sigh. "I wish I could tell you and Crystal this under better circumstances, but I'm afraid your involvement is no accident. Naarin, darling, did you ever ask yourself why you and the other Watchers were sent to protect only certain children?"

"Because they were the ones who believed in us," Naarin said, though he looked doubtful now. "At least… that's what I'd assumed. Are you telling me that's wrong?"

"I'm afraid so," Nikkela replied. "The children do not merely believe we exist; they're *proof* we do. You see, they are half-fairy, half-human."

"I should have known," Naarin said, cursing under his breath in a language I didn't recognize. "The fact you could see the Nightstalker was a hint I failed to pay any attention to."

"Wait, what are you talking about? What do you mean?" Crystal asked, giving me a confused look as she tried to take in what she was being told.

"There's a reason Nightstalkers are so effective at hunting humans," Naarin replied. "To those who aren't sensitive to magic they appear as little more than a passing shadow—they're covered in spells intended to trick non-magical minds into refusing to recognize them—but if you have fairy blood within you, it means you can see through their disguise."

"But why did my parents lie to me?" Mickey asked, shaking in shock. "Why not just tell me who they were?"

"It's possible one of your parents was unaware of the other's true nature," Nikkela replied. "I know Clint's mother was a fairy because she's my mother's sister, but I'm afraid I can't even begin to guess the story behind your or Crystal's parents."

"It's time to leave," came a voice then, cutting off any further conversation as the door opened to reveal one of our jailers. "The Queen has granted you an audience to plead your cause; you'd best follow me."

We were taken along a long, winding corridor that eventually led to a low doorway, beyond which a massive circular chamber. At its center stood the same woman we'd first met, waiting in a shaft of light that fell from a skylight in the ceiling above us. She had short, well-kept blonde hair, and her fierce-looking blue eyes watched us as we entered.

For a moment I assumed this was the Queen who had summoned us to her presence, but then the woman stepped aside to reveal a small, plain-looking throne, upon which sat a woman who appeared to be middle-aged by human standards, her graying hair half-hiding a heavily wrinkled face and a pair of gray eyes. She was wearing a long white dress, and glimmering jewels were set into the rings that adorned her fingers. We approached cautiously, unsure what to say as the guard who'd escorted us left the room again.

"The Queen of the Sidhe, Morgaen, welcomes you to her fortress," the younger woman said after a few moments of awkward silence. "My name is Neszra, I am the Queen's…companion. My apologies for the form your welcome took earlier."

"I understand the caution," Naarin said, bowing and motioning for us to do the same. "Considering the threats our world now faces, it's understandable you would wish to be cautious at the approach of strangers."

"She mentioned this…'threat'…you speak of," Morgaen said, stirring so suddenly that even her fellow Sidhe appeared to be caught off guard by the movement. "I have heard of no such battle, so explain yourselves: I'm curious to know why you think I should help you."

"There are creatures of darkness abroad in the world," Finarae replied, "far worse than any of our kind have ever faced before, and in far greater numbers. As the humans show no willingness to come to our aid, we are gathering what forces we can to attempt to fight back while we still have a chance of turning this situation around."

"And you seek my kind's aid in this endeavour?" Morgaen asked, studying the Pixie carefully. "We do not send our soldiers to war on the whims of others; if you are to receive our aid you will have to do more than simply ask politely."

"This situation is desperate," Naarin replied. "If we must pass a test in order to gain your alliance, so be it. Name your price."

"My champion here will fight a duel," Morgaen said, "and she will have the choice of who her opponent is."

"I choose *him*!" Neszra said, pointing straight at me.

"You can't do that!" Niana exclaimed, stepping in front of me. "Challenge my brother—at least he's trained as a warrior."

"I have chosen already," Neszra replied forcefully. "Your choice is simple: accept my challenge and have the chance to earn the loyalty of every warrior on this island, or refuse and you'll be kicked out of here and never be allowed to return again, no matter what happens in this war."

Chapter 8

"Naarin, do something!" Niana shouted, turning on her brother angrily. "She could kill him without even breaking into a sweat! No offence," she added, glancing at me.

"Finarae, you know the Sidhe better than we do," I said before Naarin had a chance to respond. "Tell me the truth: is there any other way of doing this?"

"I hate to say it but no," Finarae replied with a sigh. "Sidhe are big on honor and tradition; once the champion chooses an opponent, they won't change their mind."

"So, we go somewhere else," Crystal said. "I don't care who they are; nothing's worth risking his life for, no matter how powerful they are."

"So, you want us to leave?" I asked her, raising an eyebrow. "And run the risk of the enemy getting them on side? I hate this more than you do, Crystal—believe me—but I don't think we have any other option."

"At least use my sword," Naarin said, unsheathing it and passing it to me. "Your blade is hardly bad, but something tells me you could do with all the help you can get."

"Be careful," Niana said, kissing me softly on the cheek. "I don't mind you being a hero but it'd be nice if you didn't get yourself killed quite so soon after meeting each other."

"I'll do my best," I said, laughing, though it sounded a little hysterical.

I turned around to find Neszra standing there, waiting for me; she'd cast her cloak off to reveal a slim—but still imposing—suit of turquoise armor. She was carrying a short sword that extended to a razor-sharp point. She bowed slightly as I approached.

"I don't suppose there's any point in asking you to go easy on me, is there?" I asked, trying to keep my voice from wavering.

"No," the Sidhe replied, "but I will at least allow you the luxury of making the first attack."

I had to take a moment to take a deep, calming breath before I lunged for her, finding her deflecting my swing with a dismissive flick of her sword and meeting my attempt to swing back the other way with a similar move. For a time, the combat continued like this, causing me to think she was going easy on me, not that I couldn't feel my heart beating rapidly in spite of this. However, her experience soon—and inevitably—began to show as she pushed me effortlessly back toward my friends.

In the midst of the silence, I suddenly heard Niana's voice call out. "Clint, she's using her magic to make her moves quicker than your reflexes, but she doesn't know about your parentage! Close your eyes; you'll be able to see what she's trying to do to trick you."

"What are you…" I started saying, before being forced to duck under a blow aimed at my head. "Well, I guess I've got nothing to lose here," I muttered under my breath as I closed my eyes. For a few moments nothing seemed to happen, but then I began to see her movements through my eyelids, allowing me to dodge and move my own sword at just the right time. When I opened my eyes again, I found that her movements appeared to have slowed—at least from my perspective—and therefore I found myself back on the front foot, unable to pierce her defences but at least able to match her blow for blow. I felt my confidence flowing as I slowly pushed her back toward her Queen's throne.

"I'm impressed," Neszra said, a thin smile playing across her lips. "I hadn't expected you to last this long, but I am afraid we must end this here." Suddenly, I found her free hand forcing the sword from my own, before delivering a kick to my stomach that threw me violently across the floor.

As I lay there, winded, she approached, her sword still in one hand. However, rather than attacking me, she offered me her other hand. "Get up, Clint, the test is over."

"I…I don't understand," I said, allowing her to help me up. "I thought you'd challenged me to a duel?"

"That's not how the challenge works, child," Morgaen

replied. "If we based our loyalties on strength or power we would have chosen the enemy's offer. The champion chooses to challenge the weakest person because it takes no bravery to take on a challenge you believe you can win. Real courage is believing your cause is honorable enough that you put it above your own safety. I haven't seen one so willing to do so in a very long time."

"So, you're willing to offer us the help of all your kind?" Naarin asked as Niana rushed over and hugged me tightly.

"I would have to ask the leaders of the various cairns," Morgaen replied, "but once I've made a choice, they normally follow my advice. We will offer what help we can."

"I am more grateful than I can explain," Naarin said, bowing deeply. "We should leave now; I must return to my sister with the great news."

"I understand your sense of urgency," Morgaen said, standing up gingerly, "but first I would wish to share a feast with you all as a celebration of the great fae-kin of Britain and Ireland reuniting again." She smiled. "It's been far too long."

"Of course," Naarin said, smiling. "I would not wish to insult a Queen by refusing such an offer."

"That's wonderful," the Queen replied, rubbing her hands together with glee. "I would only make one more request before we eat: could I speak to the human children, alone? In my chambers?"

"Of course, assuming they have no complaints,"

Naarin said, looking to the three of us, who offered no complaint in return. "So be it, they will join you shortly."

A short time later—after Crystal had been offered the chance to check on how Nara's recovery was progressing—one of the guards led us down a flight of stairs, passing several shrouded entrances (behind which the sounds of families eating could be heard), the occasional guard who paid little heed to our group, and several locked doors whose contents we didn't dare question our guide about.

Finally, we found ourselves at a large entrance. There was a purple silk curtain pulled across it, and through this we could glimpse a small fire and the silhouette of a woman having clothes draped over her by another woman. The guard let out a loud cough.

"You may enter," Morgaen's voice came from the other side of the curtain.

The guard moved it to allow us to pass, then let it fall back into place behind us.

Morgaen was standing in the center of the room, wearing a long, snow-white dress and a small silver tiara that was perched on the top of her head. We were caught off guard when we realised her companion was Neszra, who had shed her armor and was now dressed in a simple green tunic and knee-length brown skirt. She touched a hand to Morgaen's cheek for a moment before lowering it again, bowing to us, and exiting the room.

"Please, take a seat," Morgaen said, indicating a set of small chairs positioned around the fireplace.

"Are you two…" Mickey started asking, before realising how personal his question was and trailing off. "I'm sorry, I shouldn't ask you that."

"If only my kind could be explained so simply, young man," Morgaen replied with a soft laugh. "You're right in thinking we're close, but Neszra does not show her feelings openly to many—let's just say I'm working on bringing her out of her shell." When she reached a hand out, four goblets appeared on the table, seemingly from the air around us. "Drink—it is not poisoned."

"Thank you," I said, taking a sip to find that the clear liquid tasted fruity and sweet, but unlike anything I'd ever had before. "You said you wished to see us alone?"

"Yes," she said, settling back into her own chair. "I assume you are aware of your true parentage by now?"

"That we're half-fairy?" I asked, watching her closely. "We were told that earlier. Why do you ask?"

Morgaen stared at them intently. "What if I told you there was one child that the enemy would truly fear? I've never met them, but it is said there's a child who is half-fairy, half-Sidhe, which gives them our combined strengths without any of our respective weaknesses."

"But why would that be remarkable?" Crystal asked. "You're all fairies, so surely such children are common?"

"Not as common as you'd think," the Queen replied, "though that's the fault of my kin for being so isolated for so long." She smiled sadly. "Anyway, I would ask you all to help me locate this child before it's too late."

"But what could we possibly offer?" I asked.

"As it's likely this child is unaware of its own

parentage," she explained, "it would be easier for them to meet you and slowly discover the truth, rather than confronting it with the full nature of my kind all at once. I don't wish to force you into any actions you don't wish to take, but will you help me?"

"Of course," I answered, before the others could make any reply for themselves. "We'll do whatever we can to find this kid."

"Good," Morgaen said, standing up. "Now, I believe we've left our friends waiting long enough; let us join them and partake in the great feast that awaits us."

After the meal I took my leave from the dinner hall, finding my way to a small garden on the opposite side of the hill to where we'd entered; I wanted a chance to get some fresh air and to take in everything that had happened since I'd left my house.

The garden consisted of some well-maintained grass, flowers both familiar and mysterious, and a tall tree that towered over all but the largest hills around me. It was nice and peaceful and just what I needed.

In fact, I was enjoying the still night air so much that I didn't realize I had company until I felt a gentle touch on my shoulder. I turned to find Niana taking my hand in hers.

"It's such a beautiful night, isn't it?" she asked, resting her head on my shoulder. "I'm sorry they're putting so much pressure on you; they're not exactly asking you whether you're okay with any of this."

"I don't mind too much," I said, laughing. "It's either this or doing my exams, and quite frankly, I'll take an adventure over a test any day."

Niana laughed.

I stared at the stars for a moment, deep in thought. "Niana, can I ask you something?"

"Of course, Clint," she replied softly.

"Do you want…" I stopped, trying to choose my words carefully. "Would you like to…erm…be with me?"

"Are you asking me if I want to be your girlfriend?" she said, moving her head so she could look at my face. "Yeah, I spoke to Mickey," she added, letting out a giggle. "I don't know what'll happen before this adventure is done, but," she paused to kiss me gently on the lips, "if we both make it out of this alive, I'm never letting you go again…I mean, as long as that's what you want." I hugged her tightly, holding her close to my chest before letting her go again. "I'll take that as a yes, then." She smiled. "Come on, we both need to get some sleep."

"Of course," I said, starting to turn before I found myself distracted by a glint of silver resting in the branches of the tree above. When I concentrated, I realized it was the eye of a large, crow-like bird, and almost as if it had realized I'd seen it, it took off suddenly, vanishing into the night sky above.

"Are you okay, Clint?" Niana asked, noticing my sudden distraction.

"Hmm?" I said after a moment. "Sorry, I've just never seen this many stars in the sky at once."

Appearing to believe my comment, Niana led me back inside, leaving the garden quiet and peaceful once more.

Miles away, the raven flew until it found itself in a valley. In the center of this valley was a shallow crevasse, and within that was an expansive fairy fortress. Diving into the crevasse, the raven flew past a pair of dark-robed guards and then down a long tunnel until it settled on the outstretched, gauntleted arm of a tall fairy dressed in heavily-embossed armor.

It leant close to the fairy's ear, pausing there for a moment before taking off again. Immediately, the fairy headed for the center of the chamber, where a large pool was casting an eerie green light over the nearby wall. This wall was dominated by the shadow of the cloaked figure standing at its edge.

"My lord, I bring dire news," the fairy said. "It appears the Sidhe have sided with the forces of the Glade after all. If you had allowed—"

"If I had allowed you to attempt to destroy the Sidhe," the figure said, grabbing the fairy's wrist in a vice-like grip that threatened to break the bones as if they were made of china, "then you and your men would be long dead. This is merely a setback, one we will overcome soon enough. Why don't we allow our enemy this moment of joy? They won't be having many more." With that, the figure released the fairy's wrist, the soldier letting out a whimper as the pain hit him. "Now, go—I have matters to attend to."

Once the fairy had left the chamber, the figure turned

back to the pool, its eyes suddenly glowing red under its hood. "Patience, children; the barrier will break soon, and when it does, every creature who attempted to oppose you will be yours to feed upon at will." As the figure laughed, the glow from the pit increased momentarily, revealing its contents.

Surrounded by a green, lava-like substance, there lay Clint's mother, unconscious and hurt. But this was not what the figure was interested in.

No, he was interested in her stomach, which was extended a little more than usual.

She was pregnant.

Chapter 9

As the first rays of sunlight began to intrude through the small window of the room I'd been given for the night, I took a moment to shake off my confusion as to where I was.

I couldn't help but smile slightly at the sight of Niana cuddled next to me, her hand resting on the middle of my chest, my right arm wrapped around her. For a few moments I was simply content to watch her delicate wings twitch slightly as she slept, before my mind suddenly snapped back to the strange bird I'd witnessed the night before.

While it may have been nothing to concern myself about, I decided that at the very least I should ask the advice of Naarin and the Queen, so after carefully separating myself from my sleeping companion and pulling the blanket over her to keep her warm, I crept through the curtain that covered the entrance. The outer passageway was silent, no sign of any other occupants whatsoever as I approached the ornate door to the room

Naarin had taken. I knocked on the door as firmly as I could without making too much noise, then waited as I heard some rustling and grunting from within.

"Go away!" Naarin shouted irritably. "At least let the sun rise properly before you wake up a Prince!" Undeterred, I knocked on the door again, and this time I heard the sound of footsteps approaching. Slowly, it opened to reveal an extremely tired-looking Naarin wearing a long dressing gown. Nikkela smiled at me from her place on the bed. "Clint, what could possibly warrant banging on the door at this hour?" Naarin asked.

"I need to speak to you," I replied. "Something happened last night."

"We all know my sister is with you," Naarin said, starting to laugh, though it died on his lips when he saw my expression. "You weren't talking about that, were you? Okay, give me a second. We'd better go see the Queen; by the looks of it, she may need to know about this too."

"I don't know how long it had been there," I said to Morgaen, who was sitting on her throne while Neszra stood nearby. Naarin and Finarae were also in the room. "I wouldn't even have noticed it but for its silver eyes; I've never seen a bird with eyes that color before."

"That's because it was no mere bird," Morgaen said, rubbing her chin thoughtfully. "I had thought that form of magic long gone from the fairy world, but evidently not."

"What are you talking about?" Naarin asked, echoing my own curiosity.

"What Clint witnessed was a familiar," Finarae replied. "The silver color of the eyes come from whichever magic user created the familiar—they were seeing through the creature's eyes. Most likely they were attempting to spy on the Sidhe without risking any of us detecting their presence."

"Then we need to go out and find it," I said enthusiastically. "Maybe we can find out where it came from."

"While your eagerness is admirable, child," Morgaen said, smiling slightly, "the creature is likely long gone; once they'd become aware you'd seen it, they wouldn't have risked staying long enough for any of my hunters to pursue it. I cannot even begin to guess where it returned to—I would have to have seen it to be able to track it."

"Then what do we do?" Naarin asked.

"We should tell your sister the grave news," Finarae replied. "If dark magic of this sort is in the employ of the enemy, we may need to rethink our plan; after all, we hadn't considered what magic we may face."

"We'll meet you at the gathering the Pixie Queen is organising," Neszra said. "I'll bring every soldier the Sidhe cairns can spare."

When we teleported back to the Silver Haven, we found that while we'd been away the refugees from the Glade had apparently settled into their new home quite comfortably.

Naarin and Finarae headed toward the Queen's

chambers while Nikkela and Crystal found somewhere more comfortable to place the still unconscious Nara, leaving me and Niana standing alone in the middle of the central courtyard. I shifted slightly, still getting used to the feel of her delicate hand in mine.

"At some point it'd be nice to have a bit of time to get to know you better," I said, letting out a laugh. "We haven't exactly had masses of time to do that yet."

"Are you worried I'm hiding some deep, dark secret, darling?" she asked, giving me a look of feigned shock. "I'm sure we'll have plenty of chances to get—" Her sentence was cut short by a sudden scream that rang around the courtyard. "That came from the direction Crystal was heading in," she said, frowning, "we'd better go check they're alright."

She grabbed my hand more forcefully and pulled me into the crowd, though we only got a short distance before nearly colliding with Nikkela, who'd been running in the opposite direction. "Where are you going?" Niana asked. "What's happening?"

"I'm going to find your brother," Nikkela replied, struggling to catch her breath. "Nara has woken up, and...well, let's just say she has some rather worrying news." Before we could enquire any further, she'd sprinted across the courtyard and vanished into the crowd, leaving us with looks of utter bewilderment on our faces.

"We'd better go check on her," Niana said, helping me weave through the crowd until we found the corner where Nara and Crystal were waiting. Nara was sitting up on the edge of the bed while Crystal rested her head on her shoulder. "Are you okay?" Niana asked. "We heard the scream."

"My apologies for that," Nara said, blushing slightly. "Waking up here—considering where we'd been before—was a little...surprising, to say the least. I don't suppose your brother will be joining us shortly?"

"I'm here," Naarin said as he landed next to me, followed closely by Nareena, who already looked stronger than when we'd first arrived at the Haven. "Nikkela tells me you have some important news?"

Nara nodded. "The leader of the Sidhe Great Hunt," she said, "where is he? Where did you leave him?"

"What do you mean 'he'?" I asked, giving her a puzzled look. "Neszra is the leader of the hunt."

"No, she isn't," Finarae said, walking over. "She goes on the hunt as a representative of the Queen; the leader was one of the dragonfly riders. He'll most likely be among the forces Neszra is taking to the gathering. Why do you ask?"

"Damnit, why didn't I wake up sooner?" Nara asked, slamming a fist against the mattress in anger. "He was the one who attacked me! And it's no coincidence—you see, he knows I've seen him before."

"How is that possible?" Naarin asked. "You haven't ever mentioned visiting Ireland before."

"I haven't," Nara replied, "but he's no Sidhe; he's some unusual breed of fairy capable of altering his appearance so that even fairies see what he wishes them to see. He was in a Pixie prison I visited once on one of my rare forays to Cornwall," she explained. "He knocked me out to make sure I wouldn't blow his cover in front of the Sidhe." She paused, taking a deep breath. "If he's going to the meeting place, I fear he might have some dark plan he's about to put into motion."

"And we've left Neszra travelling with him," Naarin said angrily. "Finarae, can you get us to the meeting point as quickly as possible?" The Pixie nodded. "Then we'd better leave quickly. Nareena, if we don't return by early evening you get the refugees out of here, okay? The enemy's already three steps ahead of us; we have to assume that if they discover this location, they'll attack."

"I'm coming with you," Nara said, standing up rather gingerly.

"You're in no state to fight," Naarin shot back, giving her a stern look. "I'm not risking someone who's still recovering from their wounds."

"I'm the only one who knows for certain who the traitor is," Nara insisted. "Besides, I may have a way to stop him, but only I can do it." She smiled encouragingly. "You're just going to have to trust me."

When Clint's mother had regained consciousness, she jumped up and tilted her head back, looking up at the starry night sky just visible between a pair of high rocky walls. She didn't stay like that for long, however, as a second later she was gently pushed back against the cold, smooth rock by a young man (barely into his teenage years) dressed in a long red robe. He placed a finger to his lips before she could utter a word.

"Quiet," the boy said. "I've taken a huge risk removing you from the chamber, so I advise you to keep the noise down, especially in your condition."

"What do you mean, my—" She froze then as the cloth that had been placed over her slipped away, revealing her pregnancy. "No, that's not possible! I can't be pregnant; I'd remember something like that!" She shook her head. "No, not possible…"

"He impregnated you," the boy said simply, watching her squirm at the revelation. "Not physically, though—he used some form of magic liquid I've never seen before."

"He being who, exactly?" she asked, her voice trembling as she slid her legs over the side of the makeshift bed.

"I'm not certain," the boy replied, "but I'm told his Sidhe name is Feth'rael, which translates to 'The Eyes In The Darkness'."

"How do you…" She trailed off as she watched the boy turn around, suddenly revealing a set of wings folded against his back, visible as a small bump under his clothing. She decided to take a different tack. "My name is Kira, and evidently I owe you my thanks for rescuing me from wherever I was. What's your name?"

"Not many here care what my name is," the boy said with a sigh, "but it is Marek."

"Why would fairies cast off one of their own, Marek?" Kira asked, looking at him curiously.

"What do you mean by that?" the boy snapped, turning on her. "I don't know who you've been talking to, but I'm no fairy." He stormed off toward the door before turning to face her again. "I'll return when I've completed my chores. If you value your life, I suggest you stay here."

Kira nodded, and once Marek had left the room she mumbled, "What was that about?" under her breath. A fairy who said he wasn't one but who had wings like one…and who spoke Sidhe…she shook her head. She felt like she was trying to figure out her son all over again, which was enough of a problem in itself.

She stared down at her stomach, deep in thought for a few moments. "Oh Clint, wherever you are, I hope you're safe," she said to the empty room.

Whatever this was—whatever she'd somehow got herself into—she couldn't imagine her captor had any good intentions.

Chapter 10

When we teleported to where the army was gathering, we saw Neszra already waiting for us, Finarae having gone ahead to warn her we were coming. We met on a small mound that looked down over the camp full of Pixies, Sidhe, and other fairies we'd never seen before, all of them milling around a series of small fires.

"You'd better be sure about this," Neszra said forcefully. "If this is wrong, the Sidhe may choose to desert rather than help anyone they feel disrespected by. You sure you can prove this?"

"I'm pretty certain I can," Nara replied. "I think my mother had met creatures like him before—she gave me an amulet that counteracts their morphing magic and forces them back to their true form. I tried asking her where she got it from but she wouldn't go into any details."

"Fine," Neszra said, "but if it turns out you're right you leave the interrogation to me; my kind have special… talents…for getting prisoners to tell us what we want to know."

• • •

We made it into the camp, Finarae stopping to talk to some of the Pixies as the rest of us spread out. Me and Niana ended up with Nara, who apparently felt more confident having us two with her since she still hadn't entirely recovered from her previous ordeal. We kept an eye on our surroundings but struggled to see anyone acting at all suspiciously among the horde of fairy soldiers.

"Can't the amulet help us find him?" Niana asked, one of her hands resting close to her sword. "There are hundreds of fairies here, and even if there weren't, he can change his appearance—he could walk past us undetected multiple times."

"It doesn't work like that," Nara replied, shaking her head. "Believe me, I wish it did. On the plus side, I'm assuming he thinks I'm still incapacitated, at the very least. He's not going..." She stopped suddenly, looking over to her left where a group of young fairies were playing a game of cards. One of them was looking noticeably uncomfortable, and when Nara caught sight of the unusual tattoo on his arm she whispered, "We were looking in the wrong place," as she pointed at the tall, lanky fairy. "That's him—someone stop him!"

A stone thrown in the fairy's direction missed him as he ducked deftly underneath it before sprinting for where his dragonfly was positioned at the edge of camp. His desperation to keep an eye on those pursuing him from behind, however, meant that he missed Neszra stepping into his path, who then flattened him with a punch to the chin.

"We'd better take him somewhere a little more secluded," Nara said. "We don't want him being able to slip through the crowd unseen."

"So that's what he really looks like," Neszra said as she stared down at the prone fairy; we'd moved the captive to a small clearing in a nearby forest that was just out of view of the camp, and he'd now been revealed as an incredibly thin, ragged-looking fairy with unkempt blue hair barely stretching below his forehead, his thin frame covered by bits of torn fabric. The only sign of the Sidhe disguise he'd taken before was the pair of thick leather boots on his feet. "Are you sure that will work?" she asked, pointing to the charm that had been placed around his neck, which was currently glowing with an eerie white light. "Can't he just tear it off and escape?"

"Like I said, my mother faced his kind before," Nara explained. "They call themselves Fae'lin. She said one of their own created this charm many centuries ago to stop the Pixies from being attacked by one of their armies without warning. I don't know how the magic works, but the last time I saw her she said it would work whenever I needed it to. Besides, even if he doesn't wake up groggy, there's no way he could escape all of us now that we know about him."

"Wh...what happened?" the fairy asked as he woke up, looking down at his body. Evidently, he was trying to change, but the only thing happening was the faint glow appearing around his body for a moment before vanishing. "What have you done to me, Sidhe?"

"Removed your little trick," Neszra replied as she forcibly lifted him to his feet. "So, Lord of the Great Hunt, I believe you owe us all an explanation."

"You think I'm scared of you?" the fairy asked, laughing. "You may as well kill me now; you won't ever get a single word out of me."

"I wouldn't underestimate my...talents...if I were you," Neszra said, turning to one of the Sidhe she'd brought with us. Unlike the others who were heavily armored guards, this one was short, draped in a long red cloak, and hunched over. The figure walked up to Neszra's side. "This is Bealin. She's one of our healers, but she's as good at inflicting pain as she is at relieving it." She took a step towards the enemy fairy. "I'll make you a deal: tell me what we want to know and I'll make your death nice and quick. If you refuse, I'll allow Bealin to use her abilities, making your life deeply, deeply unpleasant."

"I have spent long enough among your kin to know your tricks, child," the fairy replied with a snarl. "Do your worst; all you'll get from me is that my name is Sad'rael."

"Well, I offered you a choice," Neszra said with a sigh. "Bealin, show him what your real talent is."

The cloaked figure raised her hand, causing Sad'rael to immediately start writhing in pain, groaning loudly, and trying to lash out at invisible assailants.

"Stop this!" I said after a few moments of feeling steadily more uncomfortable. "I want the information as much as the next person, but if we do this we're no better than the enemy."

"I understand your concern, Clint," Neszra said, turning to me so Sad'rael couldn't hear what she was saying, "but Bealin isn't really hurting him; her power is the ability to make someone *believe* they're in pain. He will suffer no physical harm."

I nodded, though I still wasn't too sure about this; even if he was evil, and even if the pain inflicted on him wasn't real, it was still a hard thing to watch.

"By Feth'rael's name I surrender!" the fairy suddenly screamed. "I will tell you what you wish, but just free me from this prison!"

"By who's name?" Neszra asked, spinning around quickly. "Bealin, let him go." The fairy let out a sigh of relief, though this was only temporary as just then Neszra threw him up against a tree. "Your master, your mission, tell me everything—*now!*"

"You are so blind to what his purpose is," Sad'rael said, cackling. "You've already all but lost this race. He has her; they are almost ready for their arrival."

"He has who?"

"The boy's mother," Sad'rael replied, a grin spreading across his face as he looked at me. "The one you assumed was dead; he's had her all this time. They are in the bowl of the demon, you—" His rambling was cut short by Neszra grabbing a spear off one of the nearby guards and killing him instantly, causing a gasp of shock to ripple around the others.

"He gave us all the useful information he was going

to," Neszra said to me, bluntly. "He would have just stood there taunting you until you snapped, Clint."

"Who is he?" I asked angrily. "Who is this master he's talking about?"

"Every fairy species has a different name for him," Neszra replied. "The Sidhe name is the one he uttered as a curse, and it translates to English as 'The Eyes In The Darkness'." She sat on the ground with a sigh. "Fairies have a story of an afterlife, and Feth'rael is…well, I suppose you'd class him as the Devil. If he *is* here, now, no good news can come from this information, especially when we have no idea where to even start looking for him."

"I think I know," Crystal said suddenly. "That thing he said before you killed him, my mum used to say that when she talked of her favorite holiday spot as a child. It's the Devil's Punch Bowl—he must be somewhere there."

"We leave now," Naarin said, before I could react. "We'll go ahead. Neszra, you follow, with any other guards you can find at short notice; we just have to hope we're not walking straight into an army."

Kira lay quietly on the bed, considering her next move while she waited for her companion to return. She was convinced that she and Marek had to leave, the problem was going to be convincing him to do so.

She was so deep in her thoughts that she didn't hear the door to the room open; didn't even notice Marek's presence until his face loomed over her.

"How are you doing?" he asked, casting an eye over her stomach before stepping back, allowing her to sit up.

"I don't feel pregnant," Kira said, dangling her legs over the edge of the bed. "Then again, I'm pretty sure nothing about this pregnancy is normal, so I don't know what should or shouldn't be happening to my body."

"I feel I should apologise," Marek said, offering her a glass of water. "I shouldn't have snapped at you earlier, but I'm still not sure what made you think I was a fairy?"

"Our kin can easily recognise each other," she said, closing her eyes as a pair of paper-thin wings suddenly appeared behind her back. She sighed. "It's been too long since I've been able to openly show my wings."

"But I have no wings," Marek said. "I would know if I did."

"Do you trust me?" Kira asked, smiling when she saw him relax slightly. "Take your tunic off—if I'm wrong you can take me back to the ruler of this place and leave him to do as he wishes with me." Marek reluctantly slid the top off, and almost instantaneously a pair of Sidhe-like wings sprung from his back. "Great Gaia!" exclaimed Kira. "You're no mere fairy; you're half-Sidhe!"

"I don't understand," Marek said, looking at his wings fearfully. "Why didn't I know this? Why would my uncle hide this from me? How did I not notice?"

"I'm not sure," Kira said, trying to think as she watched the wings, fascinated. "My guess is he was trying to protect you. There are...also spells that can hide them if necessary."

"If that's true, then…" Marek paused. "I can't stay here; neither of us can."

"Can you speak to your uncle without people getting suspicious?"

"I think so," Marek replied. "Why do you ask?"

"Because we're going to need his help," Kira replied. "We won't be able to break out of here alone."

Chapter 11

We arrived at the Punch Bowl, each of us breathing a sigh of relief when it was immediately obvious the area was unoccupied.

Me, Mickey, Crystal, and the other leaders of our group remained where we'd first emerged, while a handful of scouts spread out to investigate.

"It's empty," Crystal said, looking around. "If he's really here, surely there'd be some kind of sign?"

"You're forgetting two things, Crystal," Neszra said as she tried to scan the far side of the bowl. "We're dealing with an enemy working on a fairy-sized scale, and one whose magic is almost certainly far more complex than that which protected the Shadow Glade. It's more likely we'll find it by accident than by design."

"I might have something that can help," Mickey said, pulling a pair of binoculars from his pocket and getting embarrassed at the puzzled looks this elicited from those around him. "I enjoy bird watching, okay? I find these helpful." He shrugged. "I suppose you've got a better suggestion as to how we can inspect an area this large?"

"I hate to admit it, but he has a point," I said, stifling a giggle. "This could take forever otherwise."

"Let's see if I can see anything helpful," Mickey said, putting the binoculars to his eyes and letting out a gasp just moments later. "I might have found something," he said, pointing at a place in the distance, "that tree down by the old deserted cottage…look on the lowest branch."

"I don't see…" Naarin started saying, before catching sight of the large, black shape perched on the branch. "I think that's the familiar Clint saw. But why would it be there?"

"Because that's one of the entrances," Neszra replied. "He's acting as an early warning system—if anyone tries sneaking up on it, the enemy will know within seconds."

"So, we have a problem," I said, letting out a frustrated sigh. "Even assuming it hasn't already seen us, if we can't get in that way, how the hell are we supposed to enter?"

"That kind of familiar sight isn't always active, it strains the user too much. Besides, there's always another way," Neszra said as one of the Sidhe scouts reappeared at her side. "There's a smaller entrance near us, but we can't be sure we won't be spotted, unless…" She paused for a moment, thinking, before smiling and letting out a short chuckle. "I've got an idea, but I might need your help, Clint."

"What were you thinking?" I asked, giving her a cautious look from where I was kneeling.

"If we try and enter the city, odds are the guards will rush straight to that location," Neszra explained, "unless we're able to give them the impression they were being attacked from another direction already. So, we teleport near to the other entrance, create a diversion, then teleport back here and enter *this* entrance, hopefully before they realize they've been tricked. It won't buy us much time, but it will buy us some."

"If it means we get my mum back I'll do whatever it takes," I said. "Just get me there and tell me what I have to do."

"Okay," she said, grabbing my hand before I could say anything else. My surroundings shimmered for a moment before changing completely, and looking around, I suddenly found myself beneath the leaves of the tree Mickey had seen through the binoculars.

Neszra put a finger to her lips to stop me from saying anything. "Take this," she whispered, handing me what looked like a small silver flute. "When you play it, it will make a noise that will draw the familiar's attention. Don't use it for long, though; the moment they hear the noise I guarantee we're going to have company quite quickly. Do it now."

I did as she asked without a second thought, the noise sounding less like a whistle and more like a war horn. Even as I lowered the flute, I found myself back among the others.

"Now let's go!" Neszra said as she let go of my hand. "We don't want to waste any time."

• • •

"Someone want to explain this to me?" Mickey asked after we'd taken only a matter of steps through the entrance.

A set of steps had appeared to lead underground, but instead, the ground of the bowl seemed to vanish, revealing a crevice within which was a huge circular structure. Concentric rings of stone, occasionally broken up by enclosed chambers, could be just glimpsed from above. Several fires around its edges provided light but the only things visible were a handful of guards who seemed headed in the direction of the false alarm.

"Why didn't we see even a hint of this outside the entrance?" Mickey asked, still sounding bewildered.

"I told you," Neszra replied, "our enemy is capable of magic far beyond even his own fallen fairies. Whatever he's planning here has evidently been in motion for long enough that he couldn't risk anyone—either human or fairy—discovering his secret by accident."

"How do we get in?" I asked, thinking we were wasting time.

"There's an entrance across the bridge at the bottom of this path," Neszra said, pointing to a narrow entryway guarded by two fairies. "If we can take both of them out at the same moment the alarm won't be raised; then we'll just have to figure out how to find your mother."

"You're a good archer right, Neszra?" Nikkela asked as she took her bow off her shoulder. Neszra nodded in reply. "I'll take the guard on the left, you take the guard on the right. We'll have to time this perfectly, not to mention how well we'll have to aim these bolts."

They found a rocky outcrop that was safely out of the

immediate view of their targets, aiming as precisely as they could, and without a sound both arrows were loosed, the two guards hitting the floor within seconds of each other. It was pretty impressive.

"Come on, people," Nikkela said enthusiastically, jumping over the outcrop. "We're on a clock here—don't just stand there looking all slack-jawed!"

As we slipped through the entryway, we saw solid stone walls to either side, undecorated but for the occasional lantern. I was beginning to think we'd been led on a wild goose chase when we found ourselves suddenly inside a large circular chamber, from which we could see unnaturally formed tunnels stretching off all around us. There was no clear indication of which, if any, tunnels led in a useful direction.

"Anyone want to guess which way we go?" Naarin asked. "Even if we could follow some kind of magical trail, odds are this place is so saturated in the stuff it'd be impossible to tell which routes aren't just dead ends."

"We could split up and—" Neszra's answer was cut short by the sudden appearance of a large, wolf-like creature, which immediately jumped toward Niana.

Although Naarin's lightning-quick reflexes meant he got to the wolf in time to stop it, it did manage to rake its claws across Niana's arm, causing her to fall to her knees with a scream.

"Someone help her!" I shouted, running over, and as I touched her arm, I felt my skin tingle strangely. As a strange glow passed up her arm, the wound suddenly healed. "Wha-what just happened?"

"I should have known some of my talents would pass on to my son," Kira said as she emerged from one of the tunnels. A young man followed close behind with a tall fairy dressed in a long brown tunic, a bow over one shoulder and a greatsword buckled over the other. "Not in a million years did I ever think *you* would come to rescue *me*." She ran over to me then, pulling me into a hug before I could say anything else. As she held me, I allowed myself to breathe a sigh of relief, enjoying the comforting warmth of her body. After a few moments she pulled back from the hug, looking at the others. "Who are your friends?"

"They're a mix," I replied. "Some are fairies from the Shadow Glade, others are Sidhe, and there are even some Pixies among them." I paused, realising I was speaking rather quickly. "Mum…I know everything," I said after a few seconds, "why didn't you ever tell me?"

"Because I was trying to protect you," she replied, allowing her wings to shimmer back into view. "I know I shouldn't have lied to you, and I hoped that if you ever did discover your true heritage, it would be under better circumstances."

"Having seen a glimpse of the truth I understand why you did it," I said, smiling faintly as I stared at her wings. "You should have shown me them before; they're even more beautiful than I thought they'd be."

"So is your new lady friend," she replied, nodding in Niana's direction before letting out a soft chuckle at my embarrassment. "I don't need my magic to see the bond you two share, especially considering that, as your mother, I know you better than anyone."

Suddenly, a cough came from behind her back, and she turned to introduce her own new friends. "I'm sorry, this is Marek and his uncle Marice. I owe them my life for helping me escape the cells."

"I don't mean to interrupt the reunion, m'lady," Marice said, shifting his stance awkwardly, "but their distraction will soon wear off, and we shouldn't be here when the guards begin flooding the tunnels."

"You're right," Kira said, "but we can't go back the way they came; they'll be covering the obvious exits out of here."

"I know a way out," Marek said suddenly. "I used it when I was younger, whenever I was grounded and wanted a chance to play in the sunshine. It's a long tunnel but it will bring us out further from here than either of the normal entrances will."

"Then lead the way," Kira said as we started running after him.

We'd only got a few yards, however, before the ground between Marek and my mother on one side, and my rescue group on the other, exploded upward, a huge, cloaked figure rising from within to block our path. Most of its body was hidden beneath its long, blood-red cloak, the only visible parts being a pair of piercing red eyes and a pair of heavily gauntleted hands.

"Clint, are you alright?" my mother shouted.

"We're fine," Naarin yelled back, before turning to the newcomer. "Who the hell are you and what do you want?"

"Don't you see, Naarin? It's him," Neszra said, shaking visibly as her hand reached for her blade. "Feth'rael is here."

"Very observant, fae," Feth'rael growled, "and you even saw fit to bring the children—if you give them to me, I'll take them and the mother and leave, without any more blood having to be shed."

"Don't, Clint," Naarin said, blocking my attempt to rush the creature. "His magic is far beyond you; attacking him will only get you killed." Naarin stepped toward Feth'rael, his sword drawn. "You will be taking no one, monster! Leave now and I will spare you the fate of ending up on the end of my blade."

"Interesting," Feth'rael said, seeing all the blades drawn among those around him. "You really think you would stand a chance against me?" He shook his head, as though impatient. "So be it. I have no interest in a fight. I will, however, leave you with a little…present." With that he flicked a hand, throwing my mother against the cavern wall with a sickening thud.

Feth'rael vanished just as Neszra grabbed one of her soldier's spears and threw it at him. It clattered to the ground, its target no longer there.

"Mum, stay with me!" I said, rushing over and placing a hand on her, hoping to heal her. It took me three attempts to even get the spell correct. "Me and Nikkela can stop this; you'll be fine."

"No, Clint," my mother said, blood trickling from her mouth. "You need to go; you can't save me."

"But I only just found you again," I said, refusing to

let her go, desperately trying to push my healing magic further, not caring whether this was a good idea. As I tried to keep a grip on her I realized she was almost entirely immobile, I could only imagine from the force she hit the wall with. "I'm not leaving you here to die knowing I could've done something to help."

"You don't understand," she said. "The creature inside me, Feth'rael wants it. That's what he's really seeking; you and I are simply pawns in his plan. This...thing...is bonded with my life force—as long as I live, *it* will live."

"I can't let you go," I said, tears forming in my eyes as I looked at her expanded stomach. "I need you. I...I'm scared I can't do this without you."

"I'm scared too, Clint, my darling boy," my mother said, crying as well. "No fairy welcomes death, but my mother once taught me an important lesson: love is about knowing when to let go, no matter what pain it will cause you, if the alternative is far worse." She closed her eyes then, coughing slightly before opening them again. The fact she was grimacing with pain just at the effort of coughing brought tears to my eyes. "Before you go, Clint, there is one thing you must do for me, please?"

"Whatever you ask," I replied, fighting back the sobs.

"The boy, Marek," she whispered in my ear, "there is far more to him than I think any of us realize. Keep him with you and keep him safe; before this quest is done I fear he will have a great part to play. You must help each other. Promise me."

"I'll do what I can, but—" The words caught in my throat as I felt her body go limp, and as Niana walked over and silently put her arms around me, I let out a strangled sob. The others stood behind me, silent in their shock.

We stayed like that for several seconds, while I looked at the body of my mother and tried to keep from completely falling apart.

"Prince, you need to see this," one of soldiers said nervously as he approached Naarin, a cloth-wrapped object in one hand.

"Give us a moment," Naarin said, not bothering to turn around.

"I am aware there has been a tragedy," the soldier said, "but we found this on one of the enemy's guards—he was trying to flee the base along the tunnel we entered through—and the minute I saw this I realised you needed to see it too."

"What could possibly be so ur—" Naarin stopped mid-sentence, the color draining from his face as he caught a glimpse of what was in the package. After taking a deep breath, he wrapped it up again before handing it back to the guard. "Gather the troops outside, tell them to prepare to return to the Haven. We'll join you when we're ready."

On a small pillar of rock not far from the coast of Scotland, a small cave entrance in the midst of a bird colony hid a big secret. Inside it was the entrance to a network of tunnels full of strange, almost alien-looking fairies. They were milling around in complete silence until Feth'rael suddenly materialised in their midst.

Upon seeing their leader, one of them—who was dressed in ornate silver armor—knelt in front of the cloaked figure. "My lord, we sensed the events at the Bowl," the fairy said, careful not to look up at his master. "I am sorry we did not come to your aid in time."

"This is a minor setback," Feth'rael said, stepping toward the entrance as the fairies scattered around him. "They believe the death of the child has weakened me, but they cannot begin to imagine how wrong this impression is."

"What would you have us do?" the fairy asked, his gaze still averted.

"Our work here is done, for now at least," Feth'rael replied. "Prepare to move out—we have business in the White House."

Chapter 12

With the risks of taking my mother to the Shadow Glade being too high, we decided that my mother would be buried outside the Silver Haven, and although the service of sorts was necessarily short, afterward the others allowed me a few moments' peace next to her grave. I had a feeling Naarin and Neszra were watching me close by, but I paid them no attention; my focus was on my mum.

"There should have been another way," Naarin said angrily. "There must have been some way for us to kill the creature without her having to sacrifice her life in the process."

"We couldn't risk it," Neszra said. "She knew that better than anyone. Feth'rael knew Clint's power; he was relying on him trying to heal his mother—"

"Which would simply strengthen the enemy within," Naarin said with a sigh. "Why do choices like these never offer a simple way out?"

"Life is rarely that simple, Prince," Neszra replied.

"We'll just have to hope the discovery of this boy brings *some* good news for us." Naarin nodded in response.

"This is such a beautiful spot," Niana said as she walked up to me, placing her hand in mine. "It's just a pity she didn't live to see this view with her own eyes." At that moment I turned around, burying my head in her shoulder as she wrapped her arms around me. "I'm so sorry, Clint— I can't imagine how you must be feeling right now."

"I don't know what I'm supposed to do," I said between sobs. "I thought losing her once hurt badly enough, but to have her return to me then be taken away again straight after is even worse. I feel like…like I have nothing left in this world."

"Don't say that, Clint," she said, lifting my chin with her hand and making me look her in the eyes. "You have Crystal, Mickey, and me for one thing." She paused for a moment to kiss me gently on the lips, before resting her forehead against mine. "I'm sure you have a place in the human world, and until then—or if not—you definitely have a place among my people. You are no less a fairy than I am, Clint."

"I don't feel much like one," I said with an embarrassed laugh. "Even my mum had wings; I've not got anything."

"Oh, my darling Clint," Niana said, giggling softly. "You've spent far too long reading the old human stories about fairies. I can help you, if you trust me." I nodded in response. "Close your eyes and clear your mind, this won't take long."

I did as she requested, feeling her hand as she placed

it gently on my cheek, and after a moment she removed it. "Open your eyes, Clint," she said. "I have a nice surprise for you."

"What are you—" I started saying, before turning to see a pair of wings behind me. They appeared to be much lighter and more delicate than Naarin's, and they were beautiful. "Wh...wha...why have I never seen these before?"

"Fairy wings are usually only visible when needed," Niana replied. "I also suspect that for your own sake your mother may have cast a spell to hide them, which wore out when she..." Her voice trailed off, just in time for Desha'yi to walk over. "Desha'yi," she said, "it's good to see you again, especially after what happened. Do you wish to speak to your nephew alone?"

"As much as I appreciate your concern, Niana, that's not why I'm here," Desha'yi said, smiling softly at me. "The Queen has asked the senior fairies to go to her temporary throne room for a meeting, and we all agreed that you two and your friends should join us. We have two fresh discoveries to discuss."

When we entered the room, we found it already occupied; on one side of the large table sat Nareena, while Nightshade stood a short distance behind her. The other side was occupied by Mickey, Crystal, Neszra, Nara, Nikkela, and four other fairies I'd never been introduced to. The most notable presence, however, was Marek, who was sitting nearby with his uncle and looking around him suspiciously.

Desha'yi pointed us in the direction of two chairs, Nareena giving me a sympathetic smile before clearing her throat to get everyone's attention, bringing an end to the handful of conversations around the table.

"I am sure we all share Clint's sense of loss," Nareena said, looking around the room. "While some of us may not have known Kira as well as others, it is never a happy day to lose one of our kin. However, the attack on our enemy's fortress has given us much information that we may be able to use to our advantage. Neszra?"

"There is little good news," Neszra replied, frowning. "Feth'rael's involvement in this war was something my kin had long feared but had hoped to be proven wrong about. While it appears that the plan involving Kira has ended, I fear this was but a single element of his overall strategy."

"Of course, he has other plans," Mickey scoffed. "Why would anyone put all their eggs in one basket, especially if he's going to leave his fortress so undefended?"

"I fear it's not that helpful a scenario," Neszra replied. "Feth'rael has more than the power needed to defend that fortress; I fear he simply intended to distract us from figuring out his next move. And this has now been reinforced by what Naarin's men found among the prisoners we took."

"One of the guards was attempting to remove this from the fortress," Naarin said, placing the cloth-covered item on the table before unwrapping it to reveal a circular rock. It was glowing green and was covered in some strange writing that appeared more like artwork than any mere script. "The writing on it translates—as close as we can work out, anyway—to: '*We are the children of the darkness, we will burn the barrier, corrupt your souls, and burn the world*'."

"That sounds…unpleasant," Crystal said, looking puzzled, "but what does it actually mean?"

"It means that Kira was just one of many," Neszra replied. "This rock is one of many, too, and we cannot even guess as to the location of the others. Whatever he's doing, he'll be finding a way to summon the creatures from beyond the veil, and I promise this is not good news for humans, fairies, or indeed any other creatures on this planet."

"It's not *all* bad news, however," Nareena added. "It appears, as her last act before her death, that Kira delivered to us one who can help in the coming battle. I speak of Marek."

"I don't understand," I said, looking between Nareena and Marek. "I mean no disrespect to him, but what is a fairy my age going to do that can't be done by any other person already among our allies?"

"Do you remember what the Sidhe Queen said to us, Clint?" Crystal asked. "About the child she asked us to search for?" I nodded. "Well, Marek is half-Sidhe. Now, I'm not superstitious but I'm having a hard time believing this is an accident."

"But who were his parents?" Niana asked. "Who could have a child without either of our populations knowing about it?"

"I thought I knew," said Marek's uncle, "but while Marek calls me his uncle I am merely his guardian, and having spoken to both Neszra and the Queen, I've realized the names his parents gave me were either false or have somehow been lost from the records of both royal families."

"How could that be possible?" I asked. "Why would they go to such lengths to hide who they really are?"

"We can only guess," Neszra replied, shrugging. "It may be a fear of their families being unable to accept their relationship; as much as I'd like to think all my kin would accept a fairy in their midst, some of them believed non-Sidhe were…impure. It's not a thing of pride for me. But if we could identify his parents, then—"

"What's happening to the rock?" Crystal suddenly shouted, cutting off Neszra's speech and causing everyone to turn their attention to the object, which had started glowing more brightly than before. As we all watched, wide-eyed, an image of Feth'rael suddenly appeared in the center of the table. "How the hell did he do that?"

"Ah, I'm glad to see I've inspired you to make new friends in your hour of desperation," the image said, cackling quietly. "Don't bother attempting to attack me or trying to trace me; all the magic in your little hiding place couldn't expose my location."

"If you want to taunt us, why the hell don't you come here and speak to us in person?" I asked angrily, standing up before Niana could stop me. "We'll show you just how 'weak' we really are."

"You're in no position to threaten me, child," Feth'rael

replied, turning his red eyes on me. "Besides, I'm not here to taunt you; I'm here to give you good news. Your secret world is about to be exposed to *the* world…but I fear they will turn against you rather swiftly."

"What did you do?" Nareena asked, standing up and slamming her fist on the table. "What are you really doing?"

"Didn't you read the rock, your highness?" Feth'rael asked with a cackle. "The children will soon be here, and I have to make preparations. As for what I did to the humans? Well," he laughed again, "it's remarkable how easily humans believe you to be a threat when you tell them there's a hidden army spread out across the globe." He paused, grinning. "Soon your kind will be hunted down, so now you face a choice: stop me or save them, but choose quickly. The clock is ticking, and when it stops, this whole world will burn at my feet."

Chapter 13

"He can't be serious!" Crystal shouted angrily. "How could he turn the entire human population against you?"

"I'm afraid I can understand," Neszra replied. "It is not entirely dissimilar to how the British responded when they found out about the Sidhe colonies in Ireland. Humans have a tendency to fear what they don't understand, and discovering there are armies of creatures who have hidden themselves all across the world is unlikely to elicit a positive response from many of your kin."

"There has to be a way we can stop this before the problem escalates," Nara said, rubbing her chin thoughtfully. "We can't be completely powerless, surely?"

"I might have a way," I said, finally breaking my silence. "My uncle—my father's brother—is a politician, and the Prime Minister's closest confidante. If we could get to him before it's too late, he may be able to, at the very least, get us an audience with the Prime Minister. We'd have a chance then to plead our case."

"I'm not sure how clever an idea that would be,"

Naarin said reluctantly, "but at this point I suspect my sister is the best one to ask about diplomatic choices. Nareena?"

"I'm glad you're listening to my advice for once in your life, brother," Nareena said with a gentle chuckle. "My plan is this: Neszra, Finarae, I advise you return to your peoples and warn them about what's happened. We may have to take precautions to ensure the fairy colonies aren't overrun by surprise attacks. As for Clint's suggestion, as risky as it may be, I feel it is a risk worth taking." She stood up from her seat. "Nightshade and I will accompany you, in my case to act as an envoy and Nightshade in the event of anything going wrong. And this is non-negotiable," she said, raising a hand before Naarin could protest.

"I'm coming too," Niana said. "I've always wanted to explore the human world. Besides, I'll have to meet Clint's family eventually; you've already met mine," she added, smiling at me.

"You're enjoying making him feel uncomfortable, aren't you?" Nareena asked, a smirk playing across her lips. "I know how stubborn you are, so I won't bother arguing with you. Clint, tell us where we're going and I can teleport us there instantly."

Once we'd picked up a few supplies and got ourselves ready we stood together and linked hands, a brief flash of white light heralding our arrival at a small townhouse in the middle of a thankfully quiet road. The fairies had grown to human size to try and lessen the surprise. We hurried to the gate, pushing it open, and I was pleased to note my uncle's dog was nowhere nearby—I doubted he'd react well to my new friends.

"I still don't understand why we didn't just teleport directly inside," Niana said as we approached the door. "It would've saved us some time and effort."

"More likely it would've received an angry reaction," I said, taking a deep breath in an attempt to compose myself. "How would you like it if a group of people—most of whom you didn't know—suddenly materialised in the middle of your home?" This response seemed to embarrass her enough that she offered no further comment.

Reaching out, I knocked gently on the door, and seconds later I heard the sound of someone walking up the hallway. The next moment the door opened to reveal a tall, middle-aged man in a shirt and trousers, his red tie half-done around his neck. "Uncle Nick, it's Clint," I said, trying to keep my voice level, "I'm sorry I didn't ring ahead but I didn't expect to come until a short time ago."

"You don't need to explain to me, Clint," my uncle said, drawing me into a hug and holding me for a moment. "After your father's body was found I feared the worst about you and…" He trailed off as he saw the upset in my eyes. "Oh, Clint," he added, looking behind me to the others, "you'd better come in."

We followed him into a spacious living room. It had minimal decoration, the main features being a large sofa in the center of the room and a fireplace on the far side, the mantel of which was covered in pictures of my uncle's family. There were also a couple of bookcases, full of large, old-looking volumes.

"Are you going to introduce me to your friends or do I have to guess who they are?" he asked, gesturing at the sofa.

"I'm going to," I replied as I sat down, "but Uncle Nick, you're going to have to promise that you won't overreact."

"I've already been shocked profoundly in the last few days," he replied sadly. "I doubt there's anything you could show me that would even compare."

"Well, don't say I didn't warn you," I said with a sigh, relaxing enough so my wings became visible again. I was expecting a gasp of shock from my uncle, but he seemed more amused than shocked. "Uncle, are you okay?"

"You've seen something like this before, haven't you?" Nareena asked, looking between my uncle and me.

"I have indeed," Nick said, still studying my wings. "It's a story connected to my nephew, though he's never heard it, at least in part because I'd long since feared I'd imagined the whole thing."

"What happened?" I asked keenly.

"When I was younger I was a keen horse rider," Nick started explaining. "I used to ride my horse through Parkhurst Forest at least once a week, but one day—the day after my nineteenth birthday—there was an accident. I still don't know for certain what happened, but I got knocked out and when I woke up I found four small, winged figures sitting there, watching me intently. They told me that since I'd been hurt near to their Home Glade they would watch over me until my friend found me again. I assumed I was either delirious or suffering from concussion so I didn't question what I was seeing. One of them especially stood out to me, though: there was a female among them, the most beautiful girl I'd ever seen. She stuck in my mind so much that while I was in hospital recovering I insisted on being given a piece of paper so I could draw her."

"What happened after that?" Niana asked.

"For a few years after I continued to go back to the spot where I'd seen them," Nick replied, "but I never saw them again. At least, not for several years, until I got a rather unexpected surprise." He reached into a bookcase in one corner of the room, pulling out a sketchbook and handing it to me. "The sketch in the middle of the book...well, I think you'll recognize her."

"Who could possibly—" The words died on my lips as I saw a picture of my mother—though a much younger version—her wings even more magical-looking than when I'd seen them just hours before. "You knew she was a fairy? Were you never tempted to tell your brother?"

"It never crossed my mind," he replied. "I wouldn't have anyway, but on the night he 'introduced' us, she told me that for your father's sake he couldn't be made aware of who she was until she was sure his life wouldn't be at risk." He let out a sigh. "I never got a chance to tell her, but the reason I so willingly agreed to her terms was because she was the first person I ever loved. It was the same reason I tried to find her again." He took the book from me, staring at the sketch for a moment before returning the book to its place on the shelf. "I'm guessing your friends here are also fairies?"

"They are," I said, relaxing inwardly. I thought I'd have to spend hours calming him down and convincing him of the truth. "This is Queen Nareena of the Shadow Glade, her sister Niana, and her bodyguard, Nightshade."

"It is a pleasure to meet you," my uncle said, bowing deeply in front of Nareena and then kissing her hand softly, which caused the Queen to blush deeply. "And, as much as I'd like to think you've brought a royal to my house for a social call, Clint, I'm guessing you've got a more important reason to be here?"

"Have you seen the news?" I asked, watching him closely to see how he might react.

"You mean the US President threatening to declare war on everyone's back gardens because of some old myths?" Nick replied, a short laugh dying on his lips when he realized how this would sound to his visitors. "Yeah, I heard about it. Are you going to tell me this announcement isn't what it seems?"

"We believe he's been deceived," Nareena replied. "There's a creature, who threatens both my kind and yours, who I believe is using an outbreak of war between us to stop either of us from interfering in his real plan. I'm here to stop this disaster before the damage becomes irreparable."

"Damnit," Nick said quietly. "The President is on his

way here tonight; we're holding a state dinner, and no prizes for guessing what's going to be the main topic of conversation over the main course..."

"We have to get to the Prime Minister before he does," I replied. "There must be some way we can speak to him?"

"I can teleport us wherever you wish," Nareena said. "If I come with you, I may be able to make the case more convincingly than two humans might be able to on their own."

"I suppose there's nothing to lose here," Nick said, picking up his mobile phone and dialling a number. "Scott? Hey, I don't suppose I can have a meeting with you if you have a free moment? Cool, I'll be with you shortly." He turned to Nareena. "How are you going to get there? I can't imagine you've visited 10 Downing Street before?"

"Luckily it's fairly simple," Nareena replied. "Just take my hand and imagine our destination—if you try not to imagine how the rest of it works, it's probably for the best."

The thump of our feet landing on the carpet caused a sound loud enough that a young woman rushed into the room, freezing just as her foot landed inside the room. The Prime Minister reached out for the phone on his desk.

"I wouldn't do that, Mr. Prime Minister," Niana said, stepping into the room. "Time is frozen; there's no number you could dial that would elicit a response."

"My family," Scott said, his mind racing. "What have

you done to them?" He looked at the others, relaxing slightly when he saw his good friend Nick.

"No one has been harmed," Nareena replied. "I have simply created a local area outside of the normal timestream. Once we leave, time will continue as if we were never here."

"And you trust them, Nick?" Scott asked, giving my uncle a suspicious glance. "Storming into my office unannounced hours before my meeting with the President seems…odd to say the least."

"My nephew trusts them," my uncle replied, "and as far as I'm concerned, that's good enough for me. Besides, considering you could have police and MI5 here in moments I promise we wouldn't be here if it wasn't important."

"I suppose you have me in a position where I can hardly negotiate," Scott said, indicating the chairs on the opposite side of his desk. "I just hope I don't regret this. What is so urgent that you have to stop time just to speak to me?" He raised his eyebrows, his eyes wide.

"We believe your American ally is being manipulated into making a fatal mistake," Nareena replied, getting straight to the point. "The war he wishes to declare on the fairies—on *my* kind—will not save humanity; it will merely accelerate your doom."

"What are you basing this on?" Nick asked, studying the Queen closely.

"The source of this information is a creature called Feth'rael," I said, speaking before Nareena had a chance to reply. "He wishes to distract you while he performs a dark ritual that will summon the legions of the underworld. It is only through the efforts of the Queen's brother and the sacrifice of my mother that it has been delayed for this long."

The Prime Minister was silent for a moment, looking at each of us in turn, before finally saying, "Were I to take this story as true, then surely the safest option would be to cancel the dinner and delay the President from coming here, while we make a clearer plan for confronting this problem?"

"I have no wish to speak for the Queen," my uncle replied before any of the fairies could say a word, "but the enemy doesn't know they're here; if we attempt to delay his arrival it may alert this Feth'rael creature that we've been tipped off about his real intentions."

"So, what do you suggest we do instead?" the Prime Minister asked, looking at a loss.

"Invite us to the party," Nareena replied. "I promise we won't make a scene unless the enemy makes a move first, and anyway, since I doubt Feth'rael will come himself we may be able to identify the spy in the President's entourage."

"I'm not entirely comfortable with this," Scott said with a sigh, "but I've known Nick for too many years to simply ignore his advice. I'll make sure you're all on the guest list, and you can even go ahead and find some more suitable clothes," he added, gesturing vaguely at the rest of the house. "For some reason my family has more clothes than we know what to do with."

"Thank you very much, sir," Nareena said, standing up and curtsying. "I promise you won't regret this."

A few hours later I found myself walking down the steps of the large stately home the Prime Minister used for gatherings such as this, my uncle next to me and both of us dressed in freshly ironed tuxedos.

The two female fairies had gone off to their own room to prepare, while it had been agreed that Nightshade would go "undercover" as one of the security team.

As we reached the bottom of the stairs, I finally realized the sheer scale of the party we'd agreed to attend. Most of the front section of the house's ground floor was filled with guests, ranging from celebrities I vaguely recognized through to politicians, to the unmistakably gruff voice of the King (although I couldn't see him). From the other end of the house, I could hear the noise of the staff in the kitchens, busy making meals for the large contingent of visitors.

"Just be yourself, Clint," Nick said, giving my suit one last inspection. "You and I have got the easiest jobs of our little plan; we're not trying to be anyone we're not." He shook his head. "I wouldn't want to have to lie all evening."

At that moment a soft cough behind him made him jump, and he turned to find Nareena standing behind him. She was dressed in a long white gown, with a pair of silver shoes just about visible beneath the hem, and her crown—disguised as a tiara—just visible under her fringe. "And there was me thinking you couldn't get any more beautiful, your highness," he said, bending down and kissing her hand.

"You old flatterer, you," she said, blushing bright red and seemingly admiring him herself. "I hear there's a dance going on in the ballroom, would you like to join me? I should warn you, though—I have little dancing experience." She laughed, though it was more like a girlish giggle.

"Well, my late wife used to joke I was better suited to being a dance teacher than a politician," my uncle said with a laugh. "I promise I'll go easy on you." And with that they vanished into the crowd, leaving me standing by myself.

"Well, at least my sister seems to have found someone at last," Niana said, lightly taking my hand and kissing my cheek to get my attention. She was dressed in a garment of a similar length to the one her sister wore, but this was a scarlet red, the same color as her shoes. She let out a giggle at the confusion on my face. "Come on, Clint, haven't you noticed they haven't been able to take their eyes off each other since we first turned up at his house?" Just then, Nightshade—looking slightly uncomfortable in his tuxedo—appeared at our side. "How's a night not being the Queen's guard going for you?" Niana asked him.

"We have a problem," Nightshade growled under his breath. "The President should have been here an hour ago, but according to the head of security, they've not even offered a word of explanation for the delay."

"Maybe they've changed their minds about coming

here," I said, eyeing up a nearby table filled with glasses of champagne and orange juice. "Anyone want a drink?" I asked, the only reply being a loud gasp from Niana. "What is it?" I exclaimed, following her line of sight.

The President had finally entered the building, and he was closely followed by a woman in a long gold dress that seemed to sparkle as if actual jewels had been sewn into it. A look of sheer terror was plastered across Niana's face.

"Nightshade, who is she?" I asked, guessing they'd both recognised her.

"It… it can't be," Nightshade stuttered, "Clint, that is Niana and Nareena's mother, Periarna, but…she's been dead five years; she simply cannot be here!"

"How's that possible?" I asked, watching the woman walk toward one of the dignitaries. I was in for my own shock, however, when I saw the tall, suited man who was also part of the entourage, and whose face I recognized at exactly the same instant he saw me. "*Dad?*" I shouted. "What are you doing here?"

Chapter 14

"Dad?" he repeated, giving me a puzzled look. "I don't know what you're talking about; I've never met you in my life." And with that he followed the President into another room.

"Dad, you can't just walk away!" I shouted, causing those around us to turn and look at me. I tried to follow him, but I found my path blocked by Nightshade's formidable bulk. "Let me past, I need to talk to him!"

"That would be a bad idea, Clint," Nightshade said firmly. "If my suspicions are correct, that is not your father."

"I don't care what you think!" I snapped at him. "He's my dad, and I'm going—" My speech was cut short, however, as Niana cast a spell, sending me sprawling to the floor.

The last thing I heard before everything went black was Nightshade telling Niana, "Go get your sister—she can explain this a hundred times better than I can."

• • •

I came around slowly to see Niana's concerned face looking down at me. Sitting up, I realised I'd been lying on a bed in the room me and my uncle had got changed in not too long before, Nightshade guarding the door and Nareena sitting in a chair by the room's fireplace.

"I'm sorry I had to do that, Clint," Niana said, gripping my hand, "but you were in danger of alerting the enemy to our presence."

"All I wanted was to speak to my father," I said, speaking slowly and trying to act more calmly than before. "What's so wrong with that?"

"That wasn't your father," Nareena said, getting up and walking to the foot of the bed. "Believe me, I would give anything for that to be my mother, Clint, but this is just more proof of the dark magic our enemy has at his beck and call."

"What kind of magic could do that?" Niana asked, looking at her sister quizzically.

"Humans have always had stories of something called necromancy," Nareena replied, "and in a sense that concept is similar to what I fear this magic involves. However, fairies haven't used this kind of magic openly for a long, long time, so I can't be absolutely certain of what kind of spell it is. We have two theories, though: one, Feth'rael has somehow succeeded in resurrecting them both, wiping their memories so they can't recognize any of their former loved ones—that's the best-case scenario."

"If that's the best case, what on earth's the worst case?" I snapped.

"That somehow he found our parents' dead bodies

and removed them," Nareena replied. "Remember when I said he was attempting to summon creatures from beyond the veil? Well, not all of them can take on physical forms as easily as others. If, however, they had bodies that were no longer housing living beings—"

"They'd have a body ready to be possessed," I said, my heart sinking at the realization. "We need to confront them, find out what they're doing here."

"I agree, Clint," Nareena replied, smiling a little sadly, "but we can't risk confronting them in the middle of the party. Never mind anything else; I'm unwilling to risk any collateral damage among the other guests if a fight breaks out." Just then there was a loud knock on the door. "Come in!" she shouted.

A young man peered his head around the door and said, rather sheepishly, "The Prime Minister says the dinner will be ready shortly, if you care to join us."

"We'll be right behind you," I said, before the others could utter a response. "Come on," I added, "considering my outburst, we've got enough awkward questions to deal with without them wondering why we're not joining in the celebration."

Nareena nodded. "Then let us go."

When we got downstairs, we found that most of the guests had decamped to a large ballroom in which a series of long tables had been set up. The Prime Minister and the President were seated at a table on the far side of the room, while we were seated next to my uncle at a table near the center. Nightshade joined the rest of the security team on the fringes of the room, stationed in the best possible places to keep a good lookout. As we took our seats, I was unable to keep my eyes off the President's two companions.

"You saw him too then?" Nick asked me, not diverting his attention from the food in front of him. "I'm not sure what kind of trick they're attempting to pull but I didn't believe that was the man I grew up with even for a second."

"I didn't realize you could see through magic spells, Nick," Nareena said, looking up from her own plate of food.

"I can't," he replied, "but whoever cast it evidently didn't know my brother very well. To the best of my knowledge my brother spent his whole life being right-handed, and yet…whatever that thing is…is left-handed."

"I'm guessing accuracy in every detail wasn't exactly top of their list of priorities," Niana said, taking a bite from the meat on her plate. She paused then, looking at me as she chewed. "If this is what your food tastes like, I need to spend more time in the human world!"

"Well, I'm glad to know someone appreciates my staff's cooking," the Prime Minister said, laughing as he suddenly appeared behind Nick. "Are we all doing okay?"

"The food is wonderful," I replied, the others nodding in agreement. "Give our compliments to the chef."

"I will when I get the chance," he said, kneeling down between Nick and Nareena and talking quietly so only us could hear. "Mr. President wants to speak to me after the dinner, but he's insisting I don't have anyone with me during the meeting. I assume you would advise me against entering a room alone with his advisers?"

"Certainly," Nareena said, clearly trying to think while also trying to keep a calm and collected expression on her face. "We don't want to arouse their suspicions before they even enter the room. I have a way to get us in there, but you'll just have to trust us that nothing can go wrong."

"Frankly," the PM said, "you've given me more reason to trust you on this than the President. I'll go upstairs with him once the main course is finished; follow us when you feel the time is right."

Before the meeting we took up position in the corner of the meeting room, Nareena placing an invisibility spell over us to keep us hidden. A short time later the Prime Minister and the President walked into a large drawing room on the upper floor of the house, joined only by my father, the Queen's mother, and Nightshade in his security guise. The Prime Minister poured out four glasses of wine as the President and his advisers took the seats across from his.

"So, Tom, what is so urgent you had to change your itinerary for this trip?" Scott asked, sitting down.

"I assume you heard my speech to the nation on the newly discovered threat?" the President asked.

"I did indeed," Scott replied, before getting down to business. "In all honesty I have to say I'm cautious about supporting you, for two reasons. Firstly, you clearly didn't feel it was worth warning me personally of this global threat before you made your declaration. And, secondly, I'm curious to see what evidence you actually have of this threat."

"Are you questioning my honesty?" he asked, the anger clearly rising in his voice. "Scott, have we not been friends long enough for you to simply take my word that this threat exists?"

"Just let me get this straight," Scott replied. "You're asking me to trust you that there's an invisible army whose numbers we can't even begin to guess at, and you want me to *choose* to pick a fight with them? James, I'm not sending the British Army into a war for no reason other than 'my friend's telling me to do it'."

"This is exactly what they want," my "father" said, exasperation in his voice. "They've had centuries to build up an army to attack humanity; if we sit around arguing the point, they may destroy any hope we have of opposing them."

"If there *is* an army there'll be proof," Scott said, remaining calm in the face of the President's companions' increasing exasperation. "You'll forgive me if I find it a little strange that you won't even tell me where you got the information from," he added, quite reasonably, he thought.

"I'm beginning to wonder if even the President is aware of his source," Nareena said as she suddenly appeared, human-sized, next to Scott's chair, much to the surprise of (almost) everyone in the room. She was wearing a strange amulet around her neck, and it was glowing blue. "I'd advise your friends to sit down, Mr. President—I have no intention of hurting you, but if you attack, we *will* defend ourselves."

Niana and I went to stand either side of the American delegation, while Nightshade stepped further into the room, all three of our swords visible at our sides.

"What is the meaning of this?" the President asked, looking both shocked and angry. "Some would consider this a declaration of war, and yet you claim I'm lying? You are the only deceiver here, fairy."

"I'm impressed that you've seen my kind before," Nareena said, with a remarkably calm restraint. "I can prove, however, that your source isn't giving you the reliable information you believe they are. Is your source called Feth'rael, by any chance?"

"How could you possibly know that?" the President spat angrily. "He told me he'd spent his life isolated from society."

"I know that because he is no concerned citizen," Nareena replied. "He is an enemy of every living creature on this planet; he's only stoking the fires of war to stop fairy and human alike from being able to focus on his own actions. We've already halted one of his attempts to summon the legions of the underworld; this is simply his latest attempt to stop us halting any more of his devious plans."

"His last attempt killed my mother," I blurted out before the others could stop me. "I've seen what your 'ally' is capable of first-hand."

"Kira," my father uttered under his breath, his face

changing as if he'd suddenly broken out of a trance. "Oh Clint, I'm sorry!"

"Dad?" I asked, unsure how to feel at this sudden turn of events. "I don't understand, what happened?"

"I'm not sure," my dad replied, rubbing his forehead. "After they attacked the house, I remember waking up, but…it was like I was outside of my body. I was watching what was happening but I couldn't do a thing to stop it. Oh god, the things he's made me do!" He turned to face Nareena. "There are things I fear you haven't even begun to understand yet, Queen."

"You see now, Mr. President?" Nightshade asked before anyone else could comment. "This is what our enemy is capable of. If we don't help each other, we'll all die."

"It was Periarna who—" the President started protesting, stopping when he realised Nareena's mother had vanished. "Where did she go? She can't have left this room without one of us seeing!"

"Uh, guys, we might have a bigger problem," Niana—who was now standing by the bay window—said nervously. "If we had the element of surprise, I think we've officially lost it."

We hurried over to the window, an audible gasp spreading through us all when we saw what Niana had been looking at: an army of fallen fairies were marching straight toward the house.

Chapter 15

As I looked around the room, the Prime Minister was standing next to me, slack-jawed, while the President had collapsed back into his chair, a look of shock written clearly across his face.

"Please tell me we've got a plan to get out of this?" I asked, backing away from the window.

"Our options are pretty limited, Clint," Nareena replied with a grimace. "We've got nowhere near enough weaponry to fight them and I can't teleport us all out of the building in one go. I'd struggle to do it at full strength; it would render me near comatose trying to do it with my powers diminished."

"Could you teleport groups clear, though?" Nick asked.

"In theory," Nareena answered, "but I'd need time, and I'd also need someone else to make sure I was uninterrupted."

"We could use the ballroom at the back of the house," Nick said to the two world leaders. "Nightshade, Clint, and the rest of the security guards could try and hold them off as long as they can."

"Where will we go, though?" Scott asked. "We need somewhere we can at least temporarily occupy while we regroup."

"I've got an idea," Nick replied. "There's an old farmhouse not too far from here; I drive past it a lot, and every time I do I wish I had the money to buy it. It might not work in the long-term, but it would at least give us somewhere safe to take the guests while we regroup."

"Then it's agreed," Nareena said. "And we need to move quickly—I don't want to risk the possibility of being overrun while we're still trying to get people out of here."

We wasted no time, the two leaders gathering the guests in the dining hall and explaining the plan to them as best they could. Although it took the fairies showing their wings to convince some of the guests, they were pleasantly surprised that not only were the two leaders honest about what was about to happen, but also that most of the guests seemed to trust Nareena without pause.

Those covering the escape started setting up barricades, making sure all their guns had plenty of ammo, and then Nick came over with a pistol in his hand. Smiling, he offered it to me.

"I can't take a gun," I said, briefly looking away from the window. "I can't imagine Dad would like this suggestion, anyway."

"It was your dad's idea, Clint," Nick said, pushing the

gun into my hand. "He said that if you're going to stay here with us, he wants you armed as well."

"Listen up," Nightshade—who'd been made de facto leader of the defences—said loudly before I could even really think about what Nick had said. "I have good news and bad news: the good news is that the enemy likely won't be well-armored, so a good enough shot should take them down. They do, however, make up for the lack of protection by being extremely quick, so don't waste time between bullets."

"Did you think you could get away from me that easily, Clint?" Niana said then, laughing softly at my confusion as she sat with her back to the barricade I was hiding behind. Upon seeing my expression, she added, "I'm not sitting in some old farmhouse with a group of people I don't know while you guys risk your lives for us. Besides, you might need some magical help—Nightshade's magic is limited enough; I wouldn't fancy relying on it mid-battle. No offence," she called out to her Queen's guard as she saw him shoot her a fierce glare. "I'm just hoping they don't get anywhere near close enough that we have to ask you to use your sword."

"Stop yakking and pay attention," my dad shouted from further up the barricade. "They're almost within range!"

I looked out through a gap in the barricade and felt my heart sink as the line of fallen fairies drew nearer. Seeing guns being moved into position I pointed my own pistol through the hole, trying to find the right target. Then I waited, holding my breath.

Just then the silence was suddenly broken by an immense bang that shattered all the glass in the windows, causing the defenders to duck in order to avoid the flying shards. A handful of yelps from nearby soldiers told me that not all such attempts had been successful.

"What the hell was that?" I asked no one in particular before seeing the source; just meters from the barrier was a fairy, but it looked nothing like any fairy I'd ever seen before. It had dragonfly-like wings, a huge (if almost skeletal) frame, and it was leaning on a weapon that looked part staff, part spear. Its skin was deathly pale, and it had a pair of gray, sunken eyes just visible under its wiry gray hair. I tried to shoot at it, but it moved faster than the bullet, dodging out of view. "What the hell was that?" I asked again.

"I don't know," Nightshade shouted from where he was sitting, the soldiers around us beginning to fire as the enemy got closer. "I've seen pictures of many types of fairies in my life, but that…that was something entirely new to me."

"Clint, you'd better come here!" Nick suddenly called out. "It's your dad." I looked around to see him hunched over, his hands glowing orange intermittently.

"I'm not sure what happened," my dad said as I reached him, his breathing panicked. "One of those… things…got close enough to touch me before anyone could take a shot. The minute it vanished, this started."

"Don't worry, Dad," I said, hoping he wouldn't notice the panic in my own voice. "When Nareena comes back we'll get her to teleport you to safety."

"I...I'm not sure that's a good idea," my dad stuttered.

"What do you mean?" Nick asked.

"When it touched me, it briefly gave me a vision," my dad replied. "Those creatures, they *are* fairies, but Feth'rael created them. One of their purposes seems to involve me; they've been ordered to follow me wherever I go. No matter what, they'll always find me. They also intend to turn me into a weapon," he added. "They didn't send me to the President by accident."

"Oh my god," Nick said, the color draining from his face. "Clint, they're using him as a bomb! Their plan was to get all the dignitaries in one place, then use a weapon we could never trace, wielded by a person we'd never suspect."

"Then we get you out of here," I said, grabbing his arm. "If you're not here then no one will be in danger."

"I told you, Clint, they'll follow me," he said, shaking my hand off. "You need to go; I don't know how long this will last."

"I've already lost Mum," I said, a mixture of despair and anger in my voice, tears forming in my eyes. "I'm not losing you too. We'll find a way."

"I should be dead already," my dad said, grabbing my chin and forcing me to look him in the eyes. I could see a mixture of fear and grief raging inside him. "This should never have come about in the first place, do you understand? I love you, Clint, and I've never taken the time to tell you how proud you've made me. My two consolations are the knowledge that you'll be safe, and the knowledge that I'll be seeing your mother again in the next life." He pulled me close enough to place a kiss on the top of my head. "Now, go—you aren't safe here anymore."

"The rest of the guests have been cleared," Nareena said as she reappeared in the room. "This place is about to be overrun." As she said this, she nodded toward the window frames, where the fairies were now clambering through the broken windows, their swords drawn.

"Go!" my dad said again, pushing me towards Nareena. "Get to safety while you still can. Niana, Nick—I'm trusting you to keep him safe." He turned to face me again then, smiling in spite of his tears as he said, "I love you, Clint."

"Dad, wait…" I tried to shout as Niana grabbed me before taking her sister's hand. I tried desperately to break her grip, but as the barricade became overrun by the enemy, I caught one last glimpse of my father before a bright light flashed in front of my eyes and everything went black.

When the effects of the teleport wore off, I found we were in the front drive of a farmhouse, with my group and the two leaders, the vague sounds of the others from the party coming from somewhere nearby.

"Where are we?" I asked when my senses had returned to some form of normality, looking around to see the overgrown garden of an old cottage. As I looked, I caught a glimpse of the house we'd just left in the near distance. "My dad, we have to go—" Before I could utter another word, however, there was a large flash of light and then the entire house vanished in a pillar of smoke.

I let out a sob, falling to my knees only to be caught by Niana. Distraught, I buried my face in her shoulder.

"What the hell just happened?" the US President asked, putting a hand to his forehead. "I don't get it! If I'm their ally, why did they just try to kill me?"

"I fear I have an explanation for that," Nick said, looking down at his phone with a grimace. "Apparently people are demanding that Parliament be recalled to answer for the assassination of a US President on UK soil."

"This was their plan all along," Nareena said, the realisation making her heart sink. "You were never supposed to make it out of that building alive. But why..." She paused, looking down at the ground as she tried to formulate her answer. "Mr. President, your advisers...have any of them started acting strangely recently? It doesn't have to be anything major, just something that seems out of place."

"Nothing that I can..." He trailed off then, concern suddenly crossing his face. "My vice-president. He seemed close to nervous collapse, and he'd been working so hard that six months ago I insisted he go on a long holiday, saying the rest of my staff could look after things while he relaxed. He came back after just a week. He claimed there was a family illness, but he wouldn't tell me any more and I didn't want to intrude on a private matter."

"What are you saying, Nareena?" I asked, intrigued despite everything that had just happened.

"The best-case scenario?" she asked. "Well, there are three possibilities: one, your deputy has been an agent of Feth'rael the entire time, but recent events have accelerated their plans. Two, he was in some way converted to Feth'rael's side while he was on holiday. The third is the worst possibility; that your real deputy is dead, and that the man who's been advising you is a shape-shifter designed to fool you until the trap was ready to be sprung."

"If that's true then we can't stay here," my uncle said, anger in his voice. "We have to do something!"

"The Prime Minister should return to Downing Street," Nareena said. "As far as they know he's still alive, and we simply cannot risk raising more suspicion." She took Scott's hand in hers. "I know I can't ask you to delay the discussion indefinitely, but if you can buy us some time in order for us to make a plan and do what's needed, I will be eternally grateful."

"I owe you my life, your highness," Scott replied, bowing to her. "I will do whatever I can." He looked at the rest of us. "Good luck," he added, and then headed in the direction of a car that was waiting for him.

"What about us?" Niana asked. "Clint's right; we can't stay here. Before we know it that explosion will have this place swarming with humans."

"I fear we've had to reveal ourselves to the world far sooner than I might have wished," Nareena replied sadly. "We need somewhere we can speak to the world but where we're safe from any further attack."

"The United Nations," the President said. "Most countries on Earth are represented there and weapons are all but banned inside the building. The only problem is…if

I'm officially dead I'm not sure walking in through the front door is a viable option."

"I think maybe I can help with that," came a voice from a nearby tree as a tall, thin, raven-haired girl with paper-thin wings landed in their midst. "I can get you into America the same way I got out of there."

The President sighed. "One of these days, when I tell you to stay in the house you're going to actually listen to me. You shouldn't be here."

"Mr President," Nareena said, looking between the dignitary and the newcomer, "do you mind explaining to us who this charming young woman is?"

"I'm Selina," the girl replied. "I'm his daughter." Upon seeing our expressions of confusion, she said, "Yeah, he knew about fairies before the big reveal. My father has spent my entire life hoping that if he pretended my wings—and my mother's wings—didn't exist, they'd eventually go away. Hell, I'm pretty sure if he could make my magic go away he'd take it, he's been in denial for a while."

"You said you could help us," I prompted, interrupting anyone else's attempts to comment on her statement. "What do you mean?"

"No one's sure how they came to be," Selina replied, "and they seem to pre-date anyone crossing the Atlantic, but there are a series of tunnels running under the ocean, protected by a form of magic no American fairy has ever heard of, never mind wielded in any living fairy's lifespan. I can get you in, but we're going to have to be careful, and

I suspect I won't be able to take many with me." She eyed the big group of us, her expression regretful.

"Niana, Clint, and his friends can go with you," Nareena said before anyone else could speak. "If you can't risk an army, you'll need people who can help. Clint and friends bridge the gap between our peoples, and I trust Niana to represent the Glade exiles as well as I would in person."

"What about my uncle?" I asked Nareena while looking at Nick. "What's he going to be doing during all of this?"

"The Queen needs me," Nick said as I suddenly realised the two were holding hands. "Besides, I'll be more use to Scott on this side of the Atlantic than I will if I'm in America." He took out a piece of paper then, quickly scribbling something on it before handing it over to me. "If we can't be sure who's on our side, you're better off calling this number if you're in trouble. A long time ago, an old friend of mine told me not to take important calls on government-owned phones."

"I hate to break up this touching moment," Selina said, tapping her foot impatiently, "but we'd better leave now; if we're going on an adventure, I'd quite like there to still be a country left for us to explore."

Chapter 16

I was glad to see that Selina was no less talented a teleporter than Niana's sister, and in the blink of an eye we were no longer by the old farmhouse but were instead standing in the middle of a moss-covered stone circle. My first thought was that we'd been brought to Stonehenge—a place I'd once visited with school—but this site covered a much larger space and was wreathed by a strange, fog-like substance that drifted between the stones. I couldn't help but shiver, feeling slightly reassured that Selina was the only member of the group who didn't have this reaction to our surroundings.

"I thought you said you were going to take us through some tunnels?" Niana asked. "I don't see anything around here that even looks like an entrance."

"We're dealing with fairies who could bury tunnels further below the ocean than any humans could ever reach, even with modern technology," Selina replied with a sigh. "You really think with all that effort they'd make the entrance obvious to all and sundry?"

She knelt down, touching her hand to the ground while closing her eyes, and at first nothing seemed to change, the atmosphere being no less spooky than it already was. When Selina stood up again, however, a low hiss of escaping air drew our attention to the area of grass in front of her.

It had vanished to reveal a large void, the only sign of it being anything other than a bottomless pit being the set of stairs that extended from Selena's feet and went down into the pool of darkness below. "I promise this is easier than it looks," she said, noticing the reluctance on our faces. "You'd be surprised what use magical spells can be put to in good hands."

"I don't care if we have to walk for hours in the dark," I said with a laugh, "I just want to be in the warmth. I know Britain is hardly tropical, but right now it feels like we took an unscheduled trip to the freezer section of a supermarket." And then, as if to reinforce my point, I shuddered again.

We managed to get a short distance down the steps— using the limited light provided from above—before Selina whistled for us to stop.

There was the loud sound of someone snapping their fingers, and then the cavern suddenly filled with light as though it was covered in lanterns from top to bottom. As I looked up, I realized the natural light from above the ground was fading as the grass reappeared, sliding back into place.

Once our eyes had adjusted to the sudden increased light, we all let out a gasp—where we'd expected to see the staircase continuing endlessly beneath us, there instead seemed to be barely a hundred steps before it met a rock-strewn tunnel floor, which stretched off into the distance. We'd somehow reached the bottom of the staircase in hardly any time at all.

Pillars extended to the ceiling above, appearing so tall it was difficult to believe any fairy could even begin constructing such a tunnel. It was only when we realised Selina had skipped down the stairs ahead of us that we decided we'd better stop standing around and admiring the scenery.

"I suppose that's the problem with being so familiar with this place," Selina said to the air around her as we finally reached her. "You forget it takes most people a moment for their eyes to adjust, due to its sheer scale."

"How did we travel that far without collapsing from exhaustion?" the President asked, unable to hide the sense of awe in his voice. "It looks like we travelled down far more steps than we actually seemed to."

"Whoever built this evidently realised travelling through here in real time would be a nightmare," Selina replied, "so one of the many spells they cast was to allow fairies—or a group containing fairies—to be transported through this tunnel as if it folded in upon itself. I suppose the closest comparison a human would understand is that it acts somewhat like a wormhole. I'm assuming you're not complaining that we aren't walking the entire length of the tunnel in real time? I got the impression we were supposed to be in a hurry."

"Clint's still getting used to the whole fairy magic thing," Niana said, trying to spare their human companions any further embarrassment. "You can't blame them for finding this kind of thing a little…odd. I mean, I grew up in one of the most magic-laden parts of the British Isles and even I'm having a problem getting my head around all this," she laughed, gesturing at the tunnel in front.

"Well, at least you won't have to deal with your confusion for long," Selina said, setting off in the direction of the pillars. "Unless you fancy standing around and discussing the finer points of optical illusions, that is." She let out a laugh as she heard us walking hurriedly to catch up with her.

"Clint, are you alright?" Niana asked as we reached a large empty space where the pillars were more spaced apart, noticing I'd barely uttered a word since going underground. "I don't like it when people go quiet for no good reason."

I shrugged. "I'm still thinking about those…things… that attacked the party," I replied. "It's not even the creatures themselves that alarmed me; it was the fact that even Nightshade seemed scared when he saw them. I may have misplaced my faith, but I assumed he at least would have known the way out of any danger we found ourselves in."

"What 'things' are you talking about?" Selina asked from a few yards ahead of us. "I've studied the oldest library in the fairy world—much to my darling father's annoyance—so maybe I can help solve the mystery?"

"They're hard to describe," I replied, trying to think back to what had happened without being overtaken by grief. "They looked vaguely fairy-like, but they also looked like they'd just climbed out of a grave…more zombies than living beings. It felt like the very air around them became instantly colder the minute they approached you."

"Oh…oh, that's not good," Selina said under her breath as she suddenly came to a halt.

"What is it?" Niana asked. "Have you come across them before?"

"I haven't seen one with my own eyes," Selina replied, looking at me. "I'm guessing they had dragonfly-like wings?" I nodded. "Damnit, just once it'd be nice if a horrible legend turned out to be a complete work of fiction." She sighed. "They're called Wraiths—at least that's what the ancient fairies of the Americas called them. The legend goes that there was once a great war to decide which child of a fallen king would become the new ruler of the fairies. One had vastly superior military might and should have won the war easily, but he didn't count on his brother's willingness to dabble in darker magic in order to gain any advantage possible."

"Let me guess," I said, "he made a deal with Feth'rael?"

"Got it in one," Selina replied. "Feth'rael offered him an army of magically-enhanced warriors from the land of the dead in order to win him the war, but the brother forgot to consider that the deal might have consequences.

During the final battle, the one that would decide the fate of the throne was betrayed by the wraiths. Both brothers died, and Feth'rael was on the verge of gaining a foothold in this world. But *he* hadn't counted on the fact that the two brothers had a third sibling, a younger half-sister whose origins were a little…murky, to say the least. She used all the magical strength she had to injure him, forcing him to flee, and the Wraiths vanished with him. It appears that history assumed he was all that was keeping the Wraiths alive, so when their link to Feth'rael was broken, they died."

"I'm still not clear why you seem so alarmed, darling," the President said, giving her a puzzled look.

"Because, while they're not immortal by any means," she explained, "they are impervious to most weapons you would find in this world. The only fairies who use weapons that would regularly harm them—the race that the siblings belonged to—vanished from history long before even Columbus reached the shores of the New World." She sighed, rubbing her eyes. "We'll have to find a way to deal with them, but right now we have other priorities."

"Selina's right," I said. "We need to get to the United Nations while there are still countries willing to listen."

When we got to the other end of the tunnel and climbed the stairs back to the surface, we found ourselves in the midst of a stone circle almost identical to the one we'd seen at the beginning of the journey.

A starry night sky was arrayed far above us, the only sign of any human life nearby being the distant lights of planes passing overhead. We looked around to check we weren't being followed before Selina teleported us away in a big flash of white light.

Once they'd vanished, the bushes that lined the clearing rustled, and a tall figure—dressed in a long brown cloak with a sword buckled over his shoulder—stepped out, staring at the spot the group had been standing in just moments before. He then walked to the center of the stone circle, placing his hand on the largest stone.

"My Lord, you asked me for news?" he seemed to ask the air around him. "They have returned; it is time we set our plans in motion."

Chapter 17

When we materialized, we were in a large, almost pitch-black forest illuminated only by little flecks of light—which looked like fireflies—flitting between the trunks. Other than the occasional wolf howl and bushes rustling there didn't appear to be any sign of life.

Selina started walking toward the largest cluster of fireflies, stopping when she realized the rest of us had stayed on the same spot. "You're safe here, I promise," she said. "Those things aren't animals; they're magic cast by the person we've come here to find. Just be careful where you walk, I can't promise this place is a hundred percent safe."

"Can't you at least…" I started asking before realizing she was vanishing from view, the flecks of light forming a path for us to follow. We trod carefully, looking around to admire our strange surroundings—or as much as we could while trying to avoid any potential hazards.

"You'll have to excuse my daughter," the President said, chuckling lightly. "She gets it from her mother more than me. Once she gets an idea in her head—unless you can give her a good argument for changing her mind—she'll focus on it to a scary degree."

"Do you know this place?" Niana asked, keeping a firm grip on my hand. "Even my home forest is nothing compared to this."

"I can't say I do," he replied. "Although, frankly, I think pretty much anyone would struggle to identify this place in these conditions."

"Are you guys deliberately walking as slowly as possible?" Selina moaned from somewhere up ahead.

We followed her voice, eventually finding her location: she was in a small clearing, at the center of which was a large, green-flamed fire. She was leaning against a tree, the firelight enhancing the shine of her green eyes, and sitting on the opposite side of the fire from her was an older fairy, his wrinkled forehead almost hiding his dark gray eyes and a disorganised mop of gray hair on the top of his head. His clothing mainly consisted of a plain blue tunic, and he had a long brown cape thrown over his shoulders. It was only when the fire flared up for a moment that we noticed the strange drawings covering his face, some of which looked like animals, while others were entirely unfamiliar.

"I thought we were going to the UN?" I asked. "I don't see how coming here is going to help us in the slightest."

"He's the only way we can get in there," Selina explained. "At least, the only way we can get in there without having half of the NYPD turning up to arrest us, but I should really let him explain that to you."

"My name is Herian," the male fairy said. "My kind once shared lands with the Native Americans, back when there were many more of us." He smiled briefly. "I have many talents, but only two relevant to your needs." He snapped his fingers and suddenly Selina transformed into a tall, middle-aged man—much to her own surprise, never mind our own. "I can make people see you however you wish them to," he explained, chuckling at the astonished gasps that had escaped our lips.

"That's all well and good," the President said as Selina turned back to normal and consequently breathed a sigh of relief, "but they're going to want to see our ID—if we're not on the list of delegates we'll be lucky if we're not in a New York jail within an hour of trying to enter the place."

"You're forgetting something, Mr President," Herian replied. "We magical beings can make your kind see, and indeed *not* see, whatever we wish you to." At that he glanced at Selina—who shifted uncomfortably under his gaze—before turning his attention back toward the President. "I simply need identification cards I can enchant; I'll do the rest."

"We'll come with you," Selina said as her father and Herian started to move away. "Surely if something goes wrong, we'll be in a better position if there's more of us?"

"Where we're going, if we ran into any problems, we'd need a small army to help us," her father replied. "They already think I'm dead, so it doesn't matter what happens to me, but I'm not having you risking your life unnecessarily."

"Your father is right," Herian said. "Stay here and sleep; we'll return in the morning and then we'll head out on this mission." Before Selina could attempt any further protest Herian and her father vanished, seemingly melting into the darkness rather than displaying the flash of teleportation I was used to seeing.

"He's lucky we need him," Selina growled under her breath, "'cause right now I have a strong urge to kill that damn fairy." With that she vanished into the tree line, leaving me, Niana, and my friends looking around us with a shared air of bemusement.

"There are makeshift beds all around here," Niana said. "I saw them as we were approaching this clearing." We stared at her. "What?" she asked, a note of amusement in her voice. "They're designed to be hidden from human eyes; that doesn't mean my kind can't see them. We should gather them, don't you think?"

Mickey and Crystal both let out resigned sighs before walking off, Mickey's phone screen lighting their way as they went.

Almost as quickly as we'd entered the clearing, Niana and I found ourselves standing there alone.

"I bet seeing Selina makes you wish you had a sister, right?" she asked me.

"Not particularly," I said, letting out a slight laugh. "My parents weren't without their flaws but at least I didn't have to share their attention with anyone else. Not that I'm saying Naarin and Nareena are terrible people," I added, suddenly feeling embarrassed, though that embarrassment was soon relieved by Niana giggling.

"Come on," she said, taking my hand and gently brushing my cheek with her lips. "We both need to sleep, and besides, I have an idea of how we can spend the time until the others return."

I woke up suddenly in the night, the sound of movement somewhere nearby loud enough to have interrupted a very enjoyable dream. It took a moment or so for me to remember where I was, and I looked down to find I was draped in a long emerald sheet, Niana's sleeping, blanket-covered form snuggled close to my own, which was no more clothed than hers.

My moment of remembering our shared pleasure was only temporary, however, as I heard the sound again, this time followed by a sudden burst of light coming from the direction of the fire. Fearing an ambush, I slipped out from under the cover, pulling it back over Niana before dressing myself and grabbing the sword I'd left by the bed.

Approaching the central clearing, I cautiously stepped inside to find that the "intruder" was Selina, sitting on the opposite side of the fire to where Herian had sat, her cloak pulled close around her. She was still enough it almost looked like she'd fallen asleep, but when I turned to leave again, she let out a cough.

"Don't go," she said quietly, "I could do with someone to talk to, and...well...frankly, I don't think my father would be able to listen, however much he wants to protect me."

"The look Herian gave you," I said as I sat down next to her, "and his comment about making humans see what we wanted them to...it was partly aimed at you, wasn't it?"

"It's...complicated," she said, biting her lip. "The way I feel...fairies aren't meant to feel it." She shrugged. "I've spent my whole life trying to hide it from both halves of my life."

"You can tell me," I said, resting a reassuring hand on her shoulder. "With all the stuff I've been through this last week, there's nothing you could tell me that would shock me right now."

"I...I think I was born into the wrong body," she said after a few moments. "I feel like a man, no matter how much I look in the mirror and see a girl looking back at me."

I paused for a moment, taking this in. "Have you never thought to tell your dad?" I asked, watching her closely. "I don't know him that well but I can't imagine he'd be anything less than a supportive parent, no matter how much he teases you."

"I want to believe he would be too, Clint," she replied, "but I just can't put him in the position where he has to handle that. Before all this...even now...let's just say he has more than enough to worry about without worrying about my happiness."

"But he's your father," I said, reaching out for her chin and turning her face so she was looking at me. "Your happiness will be the most important thing to him. Hiding your truth from him won't make either of you feel any better."

Selina smiled. "I see now why Niana fell in love with you," she said, pulling me into a brief but tight hug before I could say anything in response. "I was going to ask Herian to give me a male disguise but I wasn't sure he'd agree, and that's not even mentioning how Dad would respond to the request."

"That we can deal with later," her father said, suddenly entering the clearing, followed by Herian. "I'm sorry—I shouldn't have been eavesdropping, and I promise I'm not mad—but we need to wake your friends immediately."

"Why?" Selina asked, a blush just visible in her cheeks which she tried to hide behind her hands. "Couldn't you get the fake IDs?"

"It's not that," Herian replied, his expression serious. "We've come into the possession of some information that has made this situation considerably more complex than we originally thought, and I'm not sure you'll want to be involved in what comes next."

"Are you sure this is a good idea?" the man asked, hunched over the computer keyboard and squinting through his glasses in the barely-lit room. He had an email client open and was in the process of attaching a document to it. "If you're wrong then there's every chance our potential allies will be in serious danger."

"There is no other way," a figure sitting in the

shadowy half of the room replied. "I've waited too long to intervene in these events. If what I've foreseen is coming, the information in this email may save more lives than we can possibly count."

"Fine," the man said with a sigh, "but if this makes things worse, don't say I didn't warn you." He rolled his chair back, though remained seated for the time being. "I'd better get you out of here before anyone wonders what I was doing in here this whole time."

With that he hit the send button before getting up and leaving the room, his companion following close behind. He'd left the computer on to return to shortly, and at the top of the inbox, left open on the screen, was an email marked high priority from an anonymous source. It had a simple but blunt subject line:

You have two days to save New York.

Chapter 18

"We assumed that the Vice-President, after taking over my role, would have other matters to deal with," Selina's father said once we'd all gathered around the fire. "After all, if nothing else he has my 'funeral' to plan. But while we were picking up our IDs the man at the desk assumed we were there to see the President's 'special guest' speak to the Assembly."

"Crap," Mickey said, punching the ground next to him. "I don't think we need to check this guy's name to know who he's sending."

"It's not a he," James replied. "It's a she. I… accidentally…caught a glimpse of her picture; it's the same woman who accompanied me to the meeting in England."

"My mum?" Niana asked, squeezing my hand so hard from the shock that I visibly winced, causing her to give me an apologetic smile. "How can they be trying the same kind of attack as before? They can't believe we'd let them do that a second time, surely?"

"I don't think they plan on attacking," Herian replied.

"Honestly, I think this is where the enemy tries to turn the rest of the world against us. They need some kind of final proof of the threat of the fairy races, and who would know better than someone who is themselves a fairy?"

"Then we have to get there first," Selina said, "or at least be a hell of a lot more persuasive."

"Why did you say we might not want to be involved?" Mickey asked, giving Herian a puzzled look.

"Because we may have misjudged the situation," Herian replied, "and if we have, and this turns into a fight, you may need to be willing to kill the messenger." He shook his head. "I can't ask you to kill a member of your own family, I just can't."

"Whatever that...*thing*...is, it's not my mother," Niana replied, standing up suddenly. "If I have to kill it in order to save people, I'll do it. I'll do whatever it takes."

"Then we'd better go," Herian said. "Let's just hope my magic is as effective at disguising us as it used to be."

When we teleported, we made sure to go to a location a few blocks away from the United Nations building, so that we could have our disguises applied and so we could sort out our respective IDs away from any prying eyes.

Once we were ready, we looked just like any other smartly-dressed professionals about to go on their daily commute. The few signs that any of us were anything other than human had been covered up, and after one last check we stepped out into the street.

I could feel Niana's grip tightening on my hand,

making me remember that she'd never been to a human city before, never mind one the size of New York, with the thousands of people constantly milling around us. I was amazed none of us got separated from the group, and it was only the considerable height of Herian that allowed us to focus on where we were heading.

The first indication we got that we were close to our destination was the group of armed guards forming a perimeter around the square in which the UN building stood. We were forced into separate lines in order to go through the security checkpoints, but I made sure Niana stayed with me; something was making me feel uneasy and I wanted her close.

As we got through the checkpoint without any problems I could see our group ahead of us, though it took me a second to realise Selina wasn't with them. As I spun around to look, I saw her being escorted into the square by a SWAT team, while more police started to surround us. By now the people in the crowd had also realized what was going on, some of them appearing startled while others took out phones or cameras to take pictures.

"I'm sorry, guys," Selina said as we regrouped in the middle of the circle. "One of the guards had some kind of magic-negating item on him and I got too close to it."

"Drop the façade, fairy scum," the SWAT leader said, pointing his gun at Selina. "We know you're not who you appear to be—any of you—so do as you're told or we'll shoot you as hostile actors on US soil."

"Do as he says," the ex-President said, reaching out to stop me grabbing the sword at my belt. "We're here to save lives, not put them at risk. If bullets start flying innocents could get caught in the crossfire."

With a sigh Herian waved a hand, making our disguises melt away and revealing us to the surrounding—and startled—crowd.

"We've been informed you intend to commit terrorism offences," the team leader said, the guns still trained on us, one or two of their fingers straying dangerously close to their triggers. "So get down on the ground because we won't ask nicely next time".

"But we haven't done anything wrong," Niana protested as a warm light started to appear around her hands. "You're threatening us without any provocation."

"I don't need provocation," the leader replied. "You've lied to us so far; why should I believe a word you say?"

"Stand down, Mendes," came a loud voice from behind him. A man in a smart blue police uniform was striding through the crowd—which parted for him, allowing him to pass—a series of medals on his uniform showing us this was no mere beat officer. Our attention, however, was drawn more to the two people following him: one was a small woman wearing a summery dress, her blonde hair flowing down her back and a journalist's ID hanging around her neck. The other was a man who stood at more than six foot five, a long red cloak just about hiding the ornate ceremonial armor underneath. There was, however, no sign of any form of weaponry on his person. "My apologies, I had no intention of you being threatened," he said to us, "this was certainly not the order

I gave to Captain Mendes. It is a pleasure to meet you, Princess Niana."

"How the hell do you know her name?" I asked angrily, before any of the others even had a chance to speak.

"That would be my doing," the red-robed figure said, stepping forward. "I had no intention of this being the response you were met with, however." He shook his head. "In my life I've discovered humans are often prone to reacting before using their supposedly great intelligence to ascertain the truth of the situation."

"That doesn't answer my question," I responded. "You haven't given us a reason to trust you at all, whoever you are."

"I trust him," Selina said. "I've never seen an aura like his before but he's definitely a fairy." She eyed him carefully. "I don't know why, but I don't believe he's a threat to us, at least he's not threatened to kill us yet."

"Captain, your men can return to their posts now," the commissioner said, turning to face Mendes. "Don't be visible enough to cause panic among passing civilians, but be ready to respond at a moment's notice if you get the call."

Mendes nodded, saluting before signalling his men to move out.

Once they'd gone, the commissioner turned to the mysterious fairy. "Ressik, you know I'll give you any assistance I can. Tell me, what do you require?"

"We need a room where we can speak in private," the fairy replied, "and, if at all possible, I would seek an audience with the Secretary-General and at least one respected representative from every continent on this planet."

"I'll see what I can do," the commissioner replied. "I can promise you your first request, but if I were you, I wouldn't hold your breath on the second."

We soon found ourselves in one of the rooms that had been put aside for especially delicate negotiations. A large wooden table dominated the center of the room, while paintings of past guest speakers adorned the walls. The wall in front of us comprised a series of large glass windows that gave a view into the assembly chamber, and although the chamber was largely empty at that time, it was clear preparations were being made for something important. While the rest of us sat down at the table, the female journalist hovered in the corner of the room, shifting uncomfortably from one foot to the other.

"Kizzy, sit down," Ressik said, nodding at a seat next to him. "If your father believed you were in any danger from my kind do you really believe he would have allowed you to be here?"

"Who is this?" Niana asked, eyeing the woman with an air of suspicion as she took her seat. "I understand why most of us are here, but I don't understand the purpose of a journalist being involved."

"You're Kizzy McDonald, aren't you?" Selina's father asked. When she nodded, he turned to us and explained, "The talented youngest daughter of the most respected journalist of the east coast, who's hardly a slouch herself when it comes to writing."

"I'm surprised you know who I am, sir," Kizzy said, giving him a quizzical look.

"Firstly, please don't call me sir," he replied with a laugh, "as of this week I'm no longer the President—at least, as far as most people are concerned. My name's James, so you can call me that. As for how I know you, I've been a friend of your father's for longer than I care to mention. The last I heard I was still your godfather, so I've kept an interested eye on your career."

Kizzy's eyes widened; apparently, she hadn't known that little—or large—bit of information.

"Not to break up this collective backslapping session," Mickey said, letting out a slight cough to try and get people's attention, "but does someone want to explain why what felt like half the NYPD just threatened to shoot first, ask questions later?"

"As I said downstairs, that was my fault," Ressik replied. "I promise, I didn't realise they'd threaten you; I would have given far clearer instructions otherwise."

"So, you just thought you'd arrest a group of fairies in the middle of the UN building? For what?" Selina snapped. "I know I said you were trustworthy but I'm beginning to wonder if perhaps my first instinct was wrong."

"Ressik is a precog," Kizzy said, before Ressik had a chance to defend himself. "Essentially, he can see the future, but unfortunately he only sees fragments in his dreams, so he's never sure what is a mere figment of his imagination and what's a real warning."

"Two weeks ago, I began to get a very specific fragment," Ressik explained. "It was an image of New York's skyline—at least, it should have been except for the fact that huge chunks of it were missing." He shook his head as he remembered. "There were pillars of smoke rising from multiple sites across the length and breadth of the city."

"And this matters to us because…?" I asked, trying to hide my frustration.

"Because yesterday my father received this email," Kizzy said, putting a tablet computer down on the table so we could all see. On the screen was an email with the words *You have two days to save New York* in the subject line. Gasps escaped the mouths of everyone in the room. "Ressik had seen premonitions of you all coming here, and he already knew Feth'rael was trying to fool the world for some reason, but when this email appeared Ressik realized action had to be taken. *Now.*"

"All I knew was that a fairy was involved somehow," Ressik said, letting out a sigh. "I didn't for a second believe any of you would play a part—indeed, my kind have been watching British fairies for longer than I've been alive—however, I simply could not risk alerting the authorities if it was too late for them to respond to the threat. I hope you can at least appreciate that the shortened deadline meant I didn't have many choices."

"I say we trust him," Crystal said, breaking the silence that had suddenly descended over the room. "We've been saying it all along: we need every ally we can find. If you'd been told to hate someone and then they tried sneaking into the UN building unnoticed, you probably wouldn't start by asking them to politely explain what they were doing."

"I'm inclined to agree with Crystal," Niana said determinedly before the rest of us could voice an opinion. "If Ressik had ill intentions then he wouldn't have saved us in the lobby." She shrugged as though it was case closed, before asking, "But what do we do next?"

"If we are to gain an advantage in this war, we cannot afford our secrecy any longer," Ressik replied. "This is why I asked for the Secretary-General to come here; he's one of the few—along with the other representatives who might be able to convince the world to offer us aid while we still have a chance of turning this around."

Just then the door opened, and a tall African man dressed in traditional Nigerian garb. He was followed by six rather nervous-looking people—three men and three women—who shuffled into the room but seemed unwilling to approach the table.

Ressik stood up, walking over to the first man. "You must be Secretary Orji," he said, bowing deeply. "I am honored that you have graced us with your presence."

"From what the Commissioner told me, I should be thanking you," Orji replied, returning the bow. "You must excuse my colleagues' rudeness, but considering recent events they're a little…tense. If there was any way you might be able to show that you trust us, I suspect they may be willing to at least listen."

"Show yourselves," Ressik said, turning to the rest of us. "I mean, your true selves." Almost in unison everyone around the table—other than the President and Kizzy—released the enchantments they'd been using to hide their wings, eliciting a mixture of shock and wonder from the dignitaries.

The biggest gasp, however, came when Ressik released his own enchantment; while his height was left unaltered, it was revealed that he was wearing a glittering red robe and a set of bracelets on his right wrist that were encrusted with innumerable gems, at the center of which was a gem that appeared to be producing its own gleam. On top of this, sprouting from his back were a pair of wings that appeared far too delicate for a fairy of his size.

He let out a light chuckle at the look of bewilderment on Kizzy's face. "I'm sorry, Kizzy, I forgot your father is one of the few humans to have seen my true appearance, I should've warned you." He turned back to the dignitaries. "I am Prince Ressik, one of the last heirs to an ancient fairy realm that once ruled large parts of the west coast of this country. I believe I speak for both myself and Princess Niana when I say the time has come for us to stop hiding." Niana let out a gasp at this.

"But why now?" Orji asked, looking between Ressik and the rest of the group.

"Because the human race is being lied to," I said suddenly, catching even Niana off guard with my sudden outburst. "You...we...are being told that fairies want to destroy us, when our real enemy is the one fomenting this tension."

"What Clint says is true," Ressik confirmed as he made a set of seats appear out of the air, which the dignitaries cautiously sat on. "We remained hidden because our role here was to protect this world from its darker creatures. As humanity lost faith in our existence our power grew weaker, and as we grew weaker they grew stronger—until now, when we're both facing our races' potential extinction. If we don't work together, Feth'rael is in danger of winning."

"But who is he?" a Frenchman in a well-pressed black suit asked. "What does he want?"

"Feth'rael is akin to what you would call the Devil," Ressik replied. "He is the lord of the fairy afterlife. As for what he's planning, we can't be certain, but we fear he's planning a great ritual to give him an advantage that even our combined resources may find difficult to overcome."

"What's that sound?" Crystal asked suddenly, alerting us to a commotion coming from outside the door.

"Secretary Orji," said a young Australian woman who'd suddenly burst into the room, "there is something outside I think you need to see."

Orji, Ressik, Niana, and I followed her out, a sense of dread washing over me as I looked out the window: pitch-black storm clouds filled the air as far as the eye could see, occasionally lit by a strange green glow that seemed to emanate from somewhere within.

"I'm too late," Ressik said, the panic evident in his voice. "In my visions, whatever caused the destruction started with this very scene!"

"Guys, you might want to see what's happening in the chamber," Mickey shouted from the room we'd just left.

As we went back in Ressik started asking, "What are

you—" before stopping mid-sentence when he saw what was happening through the window that faced out onto the assembly floor.

The chamber was crawling with fairies, wraiths, Fenrir, and some other creatures I'd never seen before, crowding the rows of seats where the delegates would normally be seated, but our attention was mainly drawn to the figure perched on the desk at the center of the assembly, his long black cloak instantly recognizable. "Secretary, you wanted to know what kind of threat Feth'rael is?" I asked. "I fear you're about to get a first-hand demonstration."

Chapter 19

"There are people down there," Crystal said as we quickly tied to take stock of the situation, while the delegates we had been speaking to were busy desperately making phone calls. "We have to get them out!"

"I'm afraid it's not that simple," Herian said grimly. "Even if we *could* get into that room unnoticed, we're far outnumbered; they'd simply slaughter the hostages while we were trying to fight through his screen of Wraiths and Fenrir."

"Sir," the SWAT leader said as he ran into the room, "the Commissioner…one of those creatures killed him, but before he died he told us to prepare to move in on the central chamber." He glanced at him. "I assume we're storming the room as soon as we can?"

"No, commander," Ressik replied. "That would be a bad idea at the best of times; against the creatures in that room your men would be dead before they could even fire off two shots."

"Then what *are* we going to do?" I asked. "We're not

helping those people in there by standing around here talking."

"I wasn't planning to, Clint," Ressik answered, rubbing his chin thoughtfully. "Commander Mendes, I suggest you use your men to form a perimeter around the building. No one else must be allowed in or out until it's been cleared; I don't want either more enemy forces or civilians complicating matters for us."

"I think we should go down there," Crystal said suddenly.

"I hate to admit it, Ressik, but it is our only option," Herian said, nodding grimly. "We'll just have to hope we all make it out of that room alive."

They wound their way through the eerily empty corridors, past closed doors from which barely-audible noises emerged, and beyond the still forms of UN staff, killed where they stood, my friends and I having to look away from them in order to avoid becoming distressed. Selina, the President, and Kizzy were especially visibly upset at the carnage around them.

When we finally reached the doors to the central chamber, we found they were locked, but the lock was no match for a quick piece of spellcasting from Herian, forcing the doors to bang wide open.

As we stepped inside and caught sight of the scale of the challenge before us, we let out a collective gasp; we were standing at the top row where the delegates would have been sitting on any ordinary working day, and the further down the rows of seats we looked, the more hostile creatures we saw, until our gazes got to the center of the chamber where we could see fifty or so terrified hostages huddled together. The thing that caught my attention most, however, was Feth'rael himself; he'd lowered his hood, revealing a remarkably gaunt but still recognisably fairy visage, his sunken red eyes scanning the room from his perch.

Our element of surprise didn't last long, with some of the creatures closest to us starting to move in our direction, until a strange sound emanating from Feth'rael seemed to stop them suddenly.

"Leave them be, my children," he said as he stood up, his six-foot-plus height allowing him to tower over the vast majority of his troops. "I do believe they are here to negotiate their surrender."

"We're here to do no such thing!" James shouted. "We're here to rescue the hostages and put an end to your plans."

"How quaint," Feth'rael said, letting out a dismissive laugh. "Look around you, 'President'. You're outnumbered, outgunned...not to mention the fact there's a bomb in here that I could trigger with a single thought." He laughed again, waving in the direction of an area behind the podium I suddenly noticed was lit by a strange blue glow. "You are in no position to threaten me."

A ripple of screams and sobs came from the hostages at the mention of the bomb.

"Then what exactly *are* you suggesting?" Herian asked, putting a hand up to stop those of us who were armed from reacting violently. "You obviously want something from us, otherwise you'd have just killed us outright the first chance you got."

"It's less some*thing*, more some*one*," he said, raising a skeletal hand towards our group. It took us a moment to realize his finger was pointing at Crystal and Crystal alone. "I may call my soldiers my children, but she is my true child."

"That's...that's not possible," Crystal stammered, staring at Feth'rael in horror. "My mother may not have told me about my true parentage, but if I was anything like you, I'd like to think I'd have had *some* idea about it before now."

"What makes you think your mother is responsible for your fairy half?" Feth'rael asked. "It is not common for male fairies to fall in love with human women, whatever they may tell you. Now, come! We are long overdue a father-daughter chat."

"She's not going anywhere with you!" I shouted angrily. "We've seen what you do to those who become your 'friends'. You want her? Well, you'll get her over my dead body!"

"Believe me, child, I would be more than willing to arrange for such circumstances," Feth'rael said with a cackle. "If you want to test your pitiful excuse for magic against mine, you are more than welcome to try."

"Don't do this, Clint," Niana said, putting a hand on my arm. "He's more than a match for my sister; you don't stand a chance against him."

"What matters are those hostages," I said to her,

leaning over and kissing her forehead lightly. "The only chance we have of changing humanity's mind about fairies is to show that we mean them no harm. If I distract him, you may have more of a chance to rescue them." I pulled her into a long, deep kiss, which felt like it lasted an age before I pulled back. "Whatever happens, don't forget: I love you, and I'm sure that—one way or another—we will find each other again."

With that, and after seeing Crystal mouth "good luck" in my direction, I proceeded down the stairs, breathing a slight sigh of relief when Feth'rael's creatures moved aside, clearing a path in front of me that led to the evil creature himself.

A few steps from the floor, however, I stopped, feeling all the hairs on my body suddenly standing on end. The atmosphere seemed to have changed without any warning, followed by a sudden flash of light, and once it had cleared, the room had several new occupants: dotted all around me were Pixies, Sidhe, and other types of fairies I'd never seen before, but who were similar to Ressik in appearance.

"I said I was the last *Prince* of my kind," Ressik said with a chuckle as he noticed the shocked faces of those around him, causing me to turn to face him. "I never said there weren't *others* of my kind." He smiled. "Our leader heard my plea! I feared I'd lost my connection with him."

"I'm sorry we're late," Neszra said, a tall male Sidhe in polished silver armor standing a couple of paces behind her. "We got a warning New York was in danger but I thought we'd find some friends before we turned up. The Queen sends her regards, by the way."

"What were you saying about being outnumbered?" I asked Feth'rael, feeling reassured now that every corner of the room had at least one ally of mine positioned nearby. "I think it should be *you* offering to surrender to *us*."

"Really, I still have the advantage he—" Feth'rael started saying, then froze as he turned to look behind him, finding that the bomb he'd expected to see had vanished. "The darklight bomb, this is some trickery! You will pay for this!" With a wave of his hand, a spear—which appeared to be composed of darkness—flew toward me, but it was deflected at the last moment by a shield that momentarily blinded me. When my eyesight returned to normal, I discovered Nareena standing between Feth'rael and the hostages, with Marek standing next to her. He initially looked the same as when I last saw him, but on closer inspection I realized he was glowing bright green, the powerless bomb in one of his hands, and also looked as if he'd grown at least three inches.

"What...what was that?" I stammered as Niana rushed over to me.

"I have remained out of this fight long enough, Clint," Nareena said, drawing her sword and stepping toward Feth'rael. "Now, why don't you fight me if you want to prove your true power?"

"We will, soon enough," Feth'rael growled as his creatures started vanishing. "This isn't over, fairies—you may have won the battle, but this war is only just beginning." And with that the figure vanished into thin air.

"What happened to Marek?" Crystal asked as she and Finarae reached the bottom of the stairs, staring in wonder at the young man's transformation. He was now dressed in an elaborate-looking tunic, his wings flowing behind him, with an ornate blade tucked in his belt.

"It would take some explaining," Nareena replied, "but suffice to say he's always had considerable power; he just required a...well, I suppose you might call it a nudge in the right direction."

"You all need to follow me," Commander Mendes said, suddenly reappearing at the entrance to the chamber. "There's something going on outside I think you all need to see."

"I think we were safer inside," Niana murmured quietly after we'd discovered that the UN building was surrounded by civilians in dressed in a variety of clothes, ranging from suits to the occasional uniform, being held back by the SWAT team. Standing slightly apart from them was a tall man in a US Army uniform, who took a step toward us, coughing slightly. "What's going on?" Niana asked him. "Are you here to order us to hand over our weapons?"

"No ma'am," the soldier said, bowing his head slightly. "I... all of us... we're here to thank you."

"I don't understand," Nareena said. "What are you thanking us for?"

"You may not know it, but the events in the chamber were playing out on live news feeds around the world," the soldier replied. "We've seen what you did to save us, in the face of the hate and distrust we offered you. I don't know what help we can offer—I have maybe fifty men and women I can call on—but we want to do what we can."

"What's your name, son?" James asked, the young soldier looking surprised at his former Commander-in-Chief speaking to him.

"Colonel Jack Samson, sir," the man replied. "Fiftieth Armoured Infantry Brigade, based not far from New York, in fact."

"Well, Jack," Nareena said, "I think I can speak for all my kind when I say that any help you'd be able to provide will be greatly appreciated." She turned to Ressik then. "Ressik, I had hoped I'd never need to do this, but it is time to call the Fae Council—let's just hope there are enough of us to listen."

"What's going on?" I asked, noticing the sudden excitement building in the fairies around us.

"The fairy races are going to war."

Chapter 20

After spending a couple of hours in New York while Nareena and the others attempted to ascertain how much support we could muster from the human race, Nareena teleported us to a strange island, around which there was open water as far as the eye could see. Indeed, the only immediate sign of life in the area was a colony of birds perched on one of the cliffsides.

At the center of the island stood a large mountain, at the base of which was a cave opening that seemed vastly too large for any creature I could ever imagine living on the entire planet. As we walked toward it, we saw fairies slowly gathering, with others landing around us even as we approached. They ranged from small, nimble creatures who looked more akin to the old pictures of fairies I'd seen as a child, to others who made Nightshade look like a small, pitiful weakling. Amid strange languages I couldn't decipher, I caught several human accents and languages.

"I don't understand," I said, looking around at the crowd. "You said your kind was dying—that you didn't have the power to protect us—but there seem to be hundreds of you here?"

"The effect I described only impacts our powers," Nareena replied. "It won't kill us outright, but it will leave us next to undefended against whatever enemies or predators we may come across." She sighed as she looked around. "This may seem considerable to you but this is barely a fraction of the numbers we would have been capable of assembling here in past years." She allowed herself a smile as Neszra landed in front of us, followed by another Pixie who seemed considerably taller than her, his fierce gray eyes watching us from behind a long, dark-haired fringe.

"I must thank you for coming to my sister's aid, Neszra," Nareena said, shaking her hand gently. "I feared the Pixies would be too busy with other matters."

"This youngling pretty much demanded we send soldiers to help," the tall male Pixie said with a chuckle. "Despite the fact I am sure our Queen would have sent any aid you wished without Neszra's…encouragement."

"Less of the youngling, you're not that much older than me!" Neszra said with a wry smile, aiming a playful shove that the other only just avoided. "I'm afraid the Queen of Cornwall is too busy hiding our warrens to travel here herself, so she sent her son instead. I'm afraid he insists on being called Firehawk—don't ask me why," she said, rolling her eyes.

"It is a pleasure to meet you," Firehawk said, bowing to Nareena and kissing her hand. "I will try to help as much as I can; hopefully you won't wish my mother was here in my place."

"Um, I…" Nareena stuttered, her surprise at Firehawk's forwardness being interrupted by a horn blowing from near the doorway.

This seemed to be the cue for the gathering to begin as the conversations around us came to an abrupt end, the groups all slowly winding their way to the entrance.

Nareena gratefully withdrew her hand from Firehawk's grasp and started striding away. "Come on, everyone—we don't want to leave the others waiting."

Crystal, Mickey, Terry and I all found it impossible to avoid letting out gasps as the tunnel we'd entered opened out into an immense cavern.

I looked around in awe; the cavern was large enough I could barely make out its roof. The walls were covered in carvings that reminded me of those I'd seen when first entering the Shadow Glade, and which were occasionally interrupted by giant portraits of fairies dressed in regal clothing.

After a while I realised that Nareena and Niana had come to a stop near a large painting not far inside the cavern. It was of a majestic-looking female fairy, who had long red hair flowing down her back and who was leaning on a very sharp-looking javelin, a small wooden shield over her other arm. Sensing there something important about the picture, I put an arm on Niana's shoulder, causing her to lean back against me.

"This is my ancestor," Nareena said quietly. "Her name was Rosewing, and she was one of the fairy queens who had close relationships with humans; it's even said that the great Queen Boudicca gave Rosewing her weapons." She paused as she took in the painting some more. "There's an oddity to her being here, though—a meeting such as this never occurred during her lifetime."

"It's because this cavern is decorated with the greatest of our kind," said a fairy who'd approached so quietly it caught all of us by surprise, with Ressik close behind. This fairy wore a long tunic that covered the top of his brown trousers, a headband the only other clothing visible on his body. He had almost entirely gray hair, and a pair of pale green eyes that stared fixedly at Nareena. "I regret that she never saw this place, almost as much as I regret that it took an occasion such as this to see so many of my own kind in one place. Do you wish to introduce us, child?"

"This is Queen Nareena and her friends," Ressik said, bowing slightly and then introducing us all by name. "They originate from the great city of Shadow Glade, and these are the great Pixies of the south of Britain. This is Stormeye, and he is...well, we don't have any concept of kings or queens among my kind; we simply call him the Great Leader."

Stormeye bowed deeply to Nareena, who curtseyed in return, a soft smile crossing her face.

"I have heard many things of your kin," Nareena said, taking his hand and leading us all towards the central dais. "Before it fell, my city contained a library that held a book with many detailed stories of them, but the last was from near five centuries ago. I feared they had been wiped out—until I found Ressik."

"My apologies for him not making his presence known to you sooner," Stormeye said with a chuckle. "When my scouts made me aware of your sister's arrival here, I did attempt to insist he take action more speedily, but he was determined to do things his way. I have long since learned it is best not to argue with him when it comes to his visions." He smiled again, causing Nareena to smile back.

We soon found ourselves on the central dais, around which twelve chairs had been set out. While the majority of the fairies were either standing or sitting around the outer parts of the cavern, Stormeye and Nareena were shown to their seats, and joining them were Firehawk, the Sidhe Queen, and some others we hadn't seen before. When everyone was seated there was still one empty chair, the guards stopping anyone in the room from taking it.

"All of the major clans are here," Nareena murmured to Stormeye. "Why the empty seat? Who are we waiting for?"

"There is one group yet to arrive," Stormeye replied, turning his head at the sound of the door opening once again. "Ah, here they are now."

A gasp rippled around the room as a group of Fenrir—and a small huddle of fallen fairies—entered the room, the sound of weapons being drawn only stopping when Stormeye stood up and called out, "Stop this! They are no threat; I asked them to be here."

"Asked them?" the Sidhe Queen said, giving him a

puzzled look. "With all the fairy and human lives they've claimed, all the blood they have on their hands, why would you invite them among us?"

"Because not everyone believes Feth'rael's plans are for the good of any of us," the Fenrir at the head of the column replied. "We know what his true intentions are, and I promise you this: without our help, you cannot succeed."

Feth'rael was sitting behind the desk of the Oval Office, a grim look on his face as he looked around the empty room. All was silent, all was still, and, finally, he was able to think.

His quiet contemplation was broken, however, when a fairy appeared across the desk from him, the shadowy form of a Nightstalker just visible on his shoulder. He shrank back slightly at the glare Feth'rael gave him, then took a moment to calm himself before he could deliver his message.

"Our ally has failed," he said. "What happened at the UN has made other world leaders increasingly unwilling to hear your message, and the President is increasingly unwilling to list—"

"You had one instruction and you failed," Feth'rael spat out, moving across the desk quickly and thrusting his arm through the fairy's body so firmly that the fairy died instantly.

Shaking the body off, he turned to the Nightstalker.

"Return to the new President, ensure he doesn't survive long enough to disrupt our plans."

With that the creature disappeared and Feth'rael stood up and walked to the window, where even from his position he could see the protests already forming outside the White House. "So be it. America will help me conquer this world...whether the country wants to or not. The children of the underworld will rise, one way or another. And when they do," he added, looking down at his arm that was suddenly covered in strange tattoo-like markings, "this world—and every creature that opposes me—will die a slow, painful death."

Chapter 21

"At least hear them out," Niana said, catching almost the entire room by surprise with her sudden outcry. "They may be lying, but who here is willing to refuse them entry and run the risk they're telling the truth?" The response was complete and utter silence. "I assume there's one of you who intends to speak for your group?" she asked.

"They call me Ereth'al," answered the Fenrir who'd spoken first, stepping forward as the others shrunk back slightly from the obvious hostility that still hung in the air. When Ereth'al reached the dais, he made his way to the remaining chair and sat down. A pair of gloved hands reached up and lowered the hood, revealing a similar appearance to that they'd seen on other Fenrir, except this one was heavily scarred. "I am aware that my kind has done little to earn your trust, and that you are well within your rights to distrust every word I speak, but I promise you this: I wouldn't have come here if I believed there was any other choice."

"Get to the point," a fairy sitting near to the Sidhe

Queen, dressed in robes that made him appear more ninja than fairy, spat out. "We don't have time to waste on worthless apologies."

"Do you have any concept of what Feth'rael's plans involve?" Ereth'al asked.

"We believe some kind of summoning spell," said the Sidhe Queen, "but we haven't the first idea how or where."

"You are both right and wrong," Ereth'al said with a sigh. "It is not so much a summoning spell he's attempting to enact, but the preparation of stripping away the last spells guarding the realm of the living from the hordes of the underworld. The weakening of the fairy races has left the barrier on the verge of collapse, hence how he can possess dead bodies and summon the Wraiths to his side."

"But how would he do that?" Nareena asked. "If it was as simple as a spell surely he would have done it already?"

"He intends to overwhelm the barrier," Ereth'al replied. "Now that he believes he has sufficient support this side of the barrier to protect him, he's going to summon the creatures from the underworld en masse. Against a full-strength fairy species he would struggle, but we are a long way from being at full strength." He sighed, shaking his head.

"But people believe in you again," Crystal said. "If what you told us is true, surely that would boost your power enough to fight him?"

"You forget the downside to us getting stronger," Neszra said, squeezing her hand tightly. "Whatever else he is, Feth'rael is still essentially a fairy—if we get stronger, so does he."

"So, we can't fight him without the humans' help, but that helps him at the same time?" Firehawk asked. "Then what? How are we supposed to win?"

"In order to summon them he's using a network of objects," Ereth'al replied, "but I'm afraid we don't know what they are. My fellow defectors and I were employed as guards for one of his hidden enclaves but his inner circle told us that if we dared look inside, our lives would be forfeit. The only hint we ever had was a brief glimpse of a group of eggs that glowed green," he added.

"But when we found my mother she was carrying the child," I said, scratching my chin thoughtfully. "Why would he have both?"

"I can't tell you that," replied one of the other Fenrir, "but we weren't aware of your mother, what happened?"

"I played a part in foiling—one of his attempts to perform a summoning spell," I replied. "He held my mother prisoner and..." I paused, grateful for Niana putting her hand over mine, offering me support. "She claimed they'd impregnated her, that Feth'rael was going to use the child to bring something into this world."

"So, if we just locate any single women who've suddenly had unexpected pregnancies we might find where the other eggs are hidden," Mickey blurted out, instantly falling quiet when he realized almost everyone in the room had turned their attention to him. "It's just a thought," he mumbled.

"That would be good if it was true," Ereth'al said, "but if what you've told us *is* true, Feth'rael is far too smart to have made his victims easy for anyone to locate if they realize what's really happening."

"Then we have a problem," Ressik said from his place behind his Great Chief. "We don't even have the first idea where to start looking, and no idea whatsoever of how long we have before this great spell is enacted."

"I might know a way," Selina said, standing up suddenly. "I mean…it's another long shot, and I read it in a book so old there's every chance it may no longer be accurate…but…"

"A long shot is better than any other option we have right now," Niana said, trying to give her a reassuring smile. "What do you know?"

"There was a book I used to read whenever I needed to escape the nightmares of the real world," Selina replied. "I don't know why—it wasn't exactly what you'd call light reading—but it included a chapter about some of the monuments of the ancient fairy races, one of which I memorized, thinking it may come in useful one day. It was called the Star Meadow, and while the book claimed it was where all fairies drew their magic from, I assumed it must be a myth because I couldn't find any reference to it outside of that one book." She shrugged.

"I think I know where that is," James said loudly enough that even his daughter jumped in surprise. "I heard Feth'rael mention a place called the Field of Stars, though he didn't know where it was, and…well, something told me I was best off not telling him. Apparently, at least part of me was always aware I was being lied to. Anyway, I'd looked it up for myself and saved it on my tablet, but…"

He sighed as he passed a tablet computer to Kizzy. "Getting to it isn't going to be easy."

"Oh geez," she said as she studied the image on the screen. She looked up at the rest of the table. "You weren't kidding. Do you guys want the bad news or the really bad news?"

"What are you...talking..." I started saying, before trailing off when I saw an image of Fort Knox, surrounded by troops. I almost laughed. "Brilliant. So, we just have to break into one of the most heavily defended places in America—unnoticed—and survive long enough to cast a spell that will probably instantly draw our enemies' attention. Tell me there's a silver lining of some description to this huge, gray cloud?" I asked desperately.

"We can get you into there," the Sidhe Queen replied. "My kin have spent more time getting past humans undetected than any of the rest of you have, plus we have...ways...of distracting those guards. Just tell me when you're ready to leave."

"We'd better leave as soon as possible," James replied. "I can guide you through Fort Knox better than anyone else in this room."

"So be it," the Great Leader said, standing up. "We will assemble a team and head out within the hour. Everyone else, it's time we fight back in any way we can." He scanned the table, looking at every individual in turn. "Gather your armies; I suspect before this war is over, we'll have to meet our enemy in one great battle."

Chapter 22

After selecting what we hoped would be the perfect team for the operation, we set out. Nightshade and Finarae were the twin leaders of the team, along with a mix of Sidhe, Pixies, and Ressik's kin, plus Selina and Niana. Mickey, Crystal, and I had insisted on coming along in case we ran into any humans we might be able to persuade to desert their posts. Nightshade had insisted we be given more formidable weaponry and more protective armor if we were heading into what was, effectively, a battlefield-in-waiting, and I had no problems with that whatsoever.

When we arrived, we found the building surrounded by tanks, soldiers, and barbed wire as far as the eye could see, with guns pointing outward in every direction. It was rather intimidating to say the least.

"We're lucky it's night-time," Nightshade muttered, louder perhaps than he meant to. "This is even more heavily defended than we'd initially thought. I assume we have a strategy that doesn't involve us all dying rather violent deaths?"

"Can you buy us some time?" one of Ressik's kin—a small, lightly-built female named Skystar—asked.

"We should have a trick or two up our sleeves," Selina replied. "What exactly did you have in mind?"

"I can create a portal into the fortress that will bypass most of their army," Skystar replied, "but I'll need time, and protection from any distractions. Simply put, we need to divert their attention to prevent them looking this way while the spell is cast."

"Couldn't you just open the portal here?" I asked.

Skystar shook her head. "Not into a building full of hostiles where I can't be sure we wouldn't be shot dead as soon as we appeared."

"And how exactly do you suggest we keep them distracted?" Mickey asked, raising an eyebrow.

"I have an idea," Selina said, grinning slightly. "Niana, Crystal, come with me. Let's show the boys how to do this properly, shall we?"

"If you think we can help," Crystal said, sounding wary as she and Niana followed Selina.

We watched nervously from the side as Skystar started chanting, the girls winding their way toward a pair of young male soldiers who were standing slightly apart from the main group, guarding what appeared to be a stockpile of guns. At first the girls seemed to go unnoticed by the two soldiers, but then they suddenly found two guns pointed in their direction.

"Stop right there, trespassers!" the taller of the two men shouted, one of his colleagues lifting his gun and pointing it toward the group. "If you don't want a bullet putting through your skull right this instant, you'd better give me a damn good reason for being here!"

"I mean you no harm," Selina said, stepping into the patch of light in front of them, her sudden change in appearance causing a gasp to ripple through our entire group; while her hair remained almost identical, where the young woman had been standing just moments before there was now a young man so handsome, even I found myself attracted to him. As the only one she'd spoken to in the group about her secret, I realized what I was watching, and I felt a certain pride swell up inside me.

"A little birdie told me you guys were getting depressed being stuck here with no chance of having any fun, so I thought I'd help relieve your boredom. My friends could always help, of course," she added, beckoning Crystal and Niana forward.

"I'm not sure about this," one of the three men said, eyeing them suspiciously.

"We've been out here for hours without so much as a mouse appearing, we're due a break. We'll go get the others," said the smaller man, a wicked grin on his face. "Although, frankly, you'd be more than enough for me, pretty boy."

"Selina, how did you know that'd work?" Crystal said once the soldiers had left, trying to avoid the enchanting pair of eyes watching her.

"Unlike his fairies, Feth'rael's human forces are easier to read than any book," Selina replied, smiling. "That particular 'man' is as straight as an arrow, but for some reason he has a fantasy about bedding an attractive guy. I just let him see what I wanted him to see."

"You're not actually going to let them do anything to us, are you?" Niana asked as they watched a crowd beginning to form nearby.

"Of course not," Selina replied. "They may think they're in for a good time, but every soldier here is about to get a very nasty surprise." She turned back around and smiled as the man who'd been leering at her walked over, stepping up to him and suppressing an angry reaction when he landed a hard smack on her ass. "I've got a little surprise for you, Private," she whispered into his ear.

"It's like Christmas come early," he growled. "Show us what you've got."

"I'm afraid you won't like my present," she said, pretending to smile sweetly as she gripped his dog tags in one hand, before pushing her other hand against his chest.

Without warning he and the other soldiers fell to the ground, thuds all around revealing that the effect had spread through most, if not all, of the camp.

Suddenly Selina stumbled, her female appearance returning as Niana ran over to help her up. "For his own sake, let us hope his path never crosses mine again," Selina said angrily.

"What was that?" Niana asked as the rest of us approached.

"I realized that knocking some of the guards out would only risk alerting the others," Selina replied, returning the smile I gave her. "I wouldn't use that much magic at one time normally, but at least now we won't—"

Her sentence was cut short by a sudden loud bang coming from the direction of Fort Knox; it caused a shockwave that almost knocked us off our feet. "That wasn't us, was it?" Selina asked.

"No, that was something else," said the fairy trying to open the portal, frowning. "I suggest we get in there right now."

We entered the building to find a scene of complete chaos in front of us. While some of the guards appeared to have been affected by the spell Selina had cast, other victims showed clear signs of violence. No sign was forthcoming, however, as to who had attacked them. Although I felt a certain relief at not having to fight our way into the building, I couldn't help feeling alarm at the sudden and unexplained violence all around us.

"These look like the marks of a fairy weapon," Nightshade said, peering closely at one of the bodies. "However, as it seems unlikely their fae allies would turn on them, and as we certainly didn't do this ourselves, I'm struggling to find an explanation for an attack like this."

"I fear I may…have an explanation…" Finarae said between gasps, causing us to turn and see that a huge, shadowy creature had pinned her against a wall.

One of the Sidhe nearest Finarae attempted to loose an arrow at it but the creature swiped it away with little effort. A second later, another fairy—who attempted to attack more directly—was knocked off his feet with a nonchalant flick of an arm.

"Keliaz, let her go!" came a voice from further into the building, as a short, blue-haired fairy approached, his arms outspread to show he was unarmed. He couldn't help but let out a slight chuckle as the creature gave him an odd look. "They are here for the same reason we are; attacking them will do us no good."

"What in hell's name *is* that thing?" Finarae asked, looking the creature up and down once it had released her. "I've seen a lot of things in my life, but nothing that comes even *close* to that."

"It would take far too long to explain his true nature," the newcomer replied. "The simplest explanation is that he is an…automaton…given life by ancient magics long since forgotten by mortal fairies."

"Then how do *you* control it?" Mickey asked, feeling more than a little confused. "You look just as mortal as the rest of us."

"I am one of the Athyrian," the stranger replied. "My name is Elion, and I came here because my kind sensed that the walls between this world and the world of the dead were on the verge of breaking. We cannot allow this to occur. I am but the advance guard for an army that will help you stop this once and for all."

"It can't be," Selina said under her breath.

It seemed some kind of realization was hitting everyone other than Crystal, Mickey, and I, creating a confusion that was only deepened when we noticed the others all suddenly kneeling down on the ground.

"He is right that he is no mere mortal fairy, Clint," said Selina, "the Athyrian…I suppose the closest concept a human would have to them are angels." She looked up at Elion. "But what are you doing here?"

"The eggs are are hatching," Elion explained, motioning the others to stand. "Time is slowly running out to stop the hell that's about to be unleashed, but thankfully for all of us, together we'll be ready to end this, once and for all."

Chapter 23

Elion led us down to the vault that had, until recently, contained the eggs hidden in Fort Knox. All that was left of them now, however, were mere shattered egg fragments, next to one of which lay the lifeless form of a creature that appeared to be something between a werewolf and a zombie. A hole had been blasted clean through its chest. At the far end of the vault there was a brightly-lit portal, through which nothing seemed visible to us apart from vague, shadowy outlines of figures none of us could identify.

"That's Heaven?" Crystal asked, raising an eyebrow. "No offence, but I assumed the entrance would be a little more...I don't know...spectacular."

"None taken," Elion replied. "I would, however, make two points in response to that comment: one, the fairy afterlife has very little resemblance to what you would consider the afterlife. Two, this is but a portal to bring the first element of our forces through; it hardly required an elaborately decorated archway." He smiled. "I'm sorry it's not more impressive."

Nightshade interrupted, "If this is as urgent as you're telling us, then we need to get to work as quickly as we can."

"And we will, shortly," Elion said, "I must speak to the younger ones first, we have...matters to discuss."

"I'll be fine," Niana said to Nightshade, who'd been reaching for his sword, clearly feeling uneasy at the suggestion. "Considering the strength of that automaton I'm sure if he meant to attack us, he'd have done so already."

After a moment Nightshade nodded, following the rest out through the vault door, but only pulling it ajar out of paranoia it would lock behind him.

Niana turned to Elion. "You have our undivided attention, so tell us: what's so important you can't tell it to the whole group?"

"I had a premonition before I entered this conflict," Elion explained. "Well, I should say I had two premonitions in very quick succession. One of them was of the eggs hatching, hence my plan being brought forward."

"That's not telling us anything we don't already know," Mickey snorted. "What about this other premonition?"

"Unlike the eggs, this involved fragments of several different visions," Elion answered. "I don't know whether I was seeing different potential futures or if something was affecting my powers, but there was one common thread: all of you were there in what appeared to be the final battle, along with a young man I don't see among your group. Something is going to happen." He sighed as he looked at us. "I have good reason to believe that at least one of you won't make it out of the fight against Feth'rael alive, but I was unable to identify who."

"What if it's Marek?" Crystal asked. "Your mother told us to protect him no matter what."

"You don't understand," Elion said. "There is no coincidence about who I asked to remain here. There were many parts of the premonition I could make little to no sense of, but one thing I am certain of is that all of you are there and then someone dies. I feel the loss, I feel the grief, but for some reason the identity of the person who dies is hidden from my sight."

"Some would consider that grounds not to go," Niana said, her gaze flickering briefly to me. "Who would want to potentially go to their death if they already know it's coming?"

"I can't pretend I like the idea of dying any more than you guys do," Selina said forcefully, "but what's the alternative? If Feth'rael succeeds then *everyone* dies. If it's a choice between that and risking one of us, I'd still risk my own life. As the old saying goes, the needs of the many outweigh the needs of the few."

"She's right," I said before any of the others could even attempt to disagree. "Besides, we already proved in New York that just because these visions happen one way, it doesn't mean reality won't happen differently. We'll just cross that bridge when we come to it, agreed?" The others all nodded, Elion offering us what was an approximation of a reassuring smile. "Okay. So, what do we do now?"

"You'll be glad to know I have some good news to share with you all," Elion replied, "but first we need to contact some of your allies; they'll need to hear this too."

I was caught by surprise—although only temporarily, remembering I was dealing with magical creatures—when I saw that in one of the larger vaults there had gathered the astral projections of Nareena, the Sidhe Queen, and several others I didn't recognise. What truly caught my attention, however, was what covered the floor: a map of Earth that, while not to scale, did seem to fill the entire floor of the room. There were bright white pillars rising out of it in places, and Elion moved over to one that seemed to be in the midst of the Atlantic.

"What you see here is a map of the location of all the eggs—well, the ones we're aware of, anyway," Elion said. "Each one is a known nest."

"I'm counting at least twenty-five," Niana said, biting her lip. "How in Gaia's name are we supposed to stop that many from hatching? Even if we could spare every fairy, we'd still struggle."

"You don't have to," Elion replied. "I believe there is one nest that, if you could destroy it, would break the link between the underworld and the eggs and therefore protect your world from the invasion."

"I hate to sound terribly pessimistic," Selina said with

a wry laugh, "but why do I get the feeling it's not going to be as simple as walking into the nest and blowing it up?"

"We know the location," said another of Elion's kind, who'd apparently been standing in the shadows listening to us, "but the enemy isn't stupid enough to make it a case of us simply walking in and ruining his plan. It's located on this island," he added, pointing to the pillar of light Elion was standing next to. "It appears on no human map, it's surrounded by a nigh-on invulnerable magical shield, and there's only one way on and off it. There's a portal inside the White House—"

"Which just so happens to be our enemy's base of operations," Selina said with an exasperated sigh. "So, how exactly are you suggesting we even get to the portal, never mind how we actually get through it?"

"We could hit as many of the nests as we can simultaneously," Nareena suggested, rubbing her chin thoughtfully. "He'll want to spread his forces in a way that will protect them if he intends a full-scale invasion. The odds are at least some of the forces at the White House will be sent."

"And who exactly are we talking about when you speak of this group going to the White House?" Crystal asked. "We'll surely need a decent-sized team so we can deal with any unexpected surprises?"

"We already know you, your friends, Selina, and my sister will insist on going, Crystal," Nareena said with a chuckle, "and I'll send Nightshade, Marek, and his uncle to help you too, as Marek is convinced he has an important part to play in this and I simply won't send him to go up against the enemy alone."

"I feel Finarae and Nara will want to help too," the Sidhe Queen said. "Finarae wants to do whatever it takes to end this threat, and Nara…well, she loves Crystal and won't let her go into battle alone. Even if the entire Pixie colony told her she couldn't join this fight, I don't believe there's anything they could do to stop her." She couldn't help smiling at the bright red blush that had suddenly spread across Crystal's face at this piece of information.

"Now that we're sure there are those willing to fight for the forces of good, my kind will provide what forces we can," Elion said. "Plus, we're also able to offer your forces a gift." He reached out, and a series of swords—all of them glowing an eerie white color—suddenly appeared on the floor, seemingly having come out of thin air. "I've heard that you believe the Wraiths can't die, well, these blades are enchanted with the same form of magic that created them. We will provide as many as you require."

"Well, I feel slightly less like I'm making the worst mistake of my life now," Mickey said, letting out a nervous laugh

"I wouldn't get over-confident, Mickey," Selina said with a wry smile. "Now begins the hardest part of all."

Chapter 24

Our small strike team—reinforced by fairies, Pixies, and a handful of Elion's men—teleported as close to the White House as we could, though I was disappointed to discover this wasn't close at all. The city was in flames, fallen fairies and Wraiths patrolling the streets, and the only signs of human life were the occasional faces that peered out from between drawn curtains.

We edged forward, trying to avoid direct conflict but keeping an eye open in case any civilian needed rescuing, and making sure to avoid the patrols raising the alarm. While most of us were evenly spaced out, Niana insisted on sticking close to me, although I had to admit I was glad she was nearby.

Elion's prediction had evidently put all of us—well, the ones he'd warned—on edge, although we were doing our best to hide it from the others.

Suddenly, Nightshade—who was at the front with Selina—put his hand up, causing all of us to stop at once.

Me, Niana, Mickey, Crystal, and Finarae crawled over to see what had caused the sudden halt, and when we reached the top of a hill from which we could see the grounds of the White House and the road in front, we realised it was crawling with troops, while burning cars and dead bodies littered the road outside the gates.

"Either we lost our element of surprise or there are more soldiers in Feth'rael's army than we realized," Nightshade said with a sigh. "There's no way we can sneak past that many."

"Could you do what you did at Fort Knox?" Mickey asked Selina, without diverting his attention from the scene in front of us. "That would make this a hell of a lot easier."

"That spell took far too much energy," Selina replied, shaking her head. "Never mind the fact there were far fewer people to knock out at once, plus the luck of a creep of a guard…no, trying to maintain that disguise takes too much of my strength to perform two spells at once."

"We knew this wasn't going to be simple," Niana said with a sad smile. "I guess we'll just have to fight our way into it." She looked at me and then the others. "Come on, the chance to save the world is waiting for us."

"Less talking, more doing," Mickey said, "we can use the cars as something approaching cover." He took off as soon as he'd finished speaking, forcing the rest of us to follow behind as quickly as we could.

Those of us with the magical blades Elion had provided kept one hand on them at all times, well aware of the likelihood of us facing Wraiths at some point during this battle.

Approaching the gates was almost akin to an obstacle course, avoiding both armed guards and civilians who might raise the alarm. When we peeked through them from behind the wall we saw that the enemy had dug trenches all the way toward the entrance of the structure. There was no obvious way across a lawn covered in trenches, but Nightshade was scanning the scene, evidently formulating a plan in his mind.

"Seraph," he said, turning to one of Elion's soldiers, "could you and your fellow creatures keep the Wraiths distracted while we fight our way into the building?"

"I'm not sure we can pin them all down," Seraph replied, "but we'll keep as many as we can from obstructing your progress."

"That's all we can ask," said Nightshade, flashing him a rare and appreciative smile as we started moving out from behind the cover of the border wall, breathing a sigh of relief the gates were already open.

Suddenly the air was filled with the sound of arrows whizzing past us, a collective sigh of relief escaping our lips as we realised the majority were being fired from our side toward the suddenly alert guards.

Nightshade had stabbed the first guard we reached but too late to stop him from shouting the alarm, battle being met violently as even Marek used either weapons or magic to fight the enemy. Niana and I were fighting side by side, and when a Fenrir got near enough to attempt slashing at my face, it found itself being beheaded thanks to a skilful swing from Niana.

"Not sure what my parents would think if they could see me here now," Mickey said, catching me by surprise as I realised his fairy wings were suddenly visible. "I mean, my dad's family have a tradition of soldiering, but I'm fairly sure he wouldn't want me on the front line."

"Well, if we make it out of here, I'm sure he won't complain too loudly," Niana said, narrowly avoiding a sword that was aimed at her stomach. "You're going to be the most popular bachelor in the world after this, I suspect."

"Selina!" Marek shouted suddenly. I turned, having a momentary flashback to what happened to my father.

Selina was on her knees, a hand to one side of her head, as Marek's uncle and Finarae defended her from attack. Mickey, Niana, and I rushed to her side, Nightshade quickly following to add to the defence.

"What's wrong, Selina?" Niana asked, lifting her head.

"I was trying to see if I could sense where Feth'rael was," Selina replied. "There's some pretty strong magic surrounding the building but I'm almost certain he's in there." She paused to take in some much-needed air. "I fear the summoning ritual is further along than we thought; we need to get in there *now!*"

"I can teleport us," Finarae said as she flattened a fairy who'd gotten too close. "I won't be able to get us far with all the magical interference, but I can at least get us into the building."

"That's good enough for me," I said as Marek, his

uncle, and Crystal joined us. "Now brace yourselves—we don't know what's waiting for us in there."

We had to hold our breath for a moment as we appeared inside the building, the stench of death permeating the place stronger than anything I'd ever smelled before, somehow even worse than at Fort Knox. Soldiers and federal agents accounted for most of the dead, although the occasional body of one of Feth'rael's allies could be seen among the corpses.

It was easy to feel the magic humming in the air around us as we stepped forward cautiously, uncertain of which direction to head in. I felt more than a little disoriented. The sensation was so overwhelming that for a few moments I felt nauseous enough to fear I was about to vomit.

"I can get us there...I think," said Selina, who still looked in a bad way. "Most of the magic in this building is focused in one room, but I'm guessing that's where most of the guards are too."

"I'm afraid your journey ends here," came a voice from behind us, and when I turned, I saw it was a Wraith who had Marek in a vice-like grip, a knife resting across his throat. "Order your forces to withdraw from this battle now!"

"Like hell we're going to do that," Selina growled, drawing her sword. "You're outnumbered; we could kill you without a second's thought."

"You forget: your human weapons are no use against

me," the Wraith said, laughing. "And those pretty trinkets can't hit me without hitting him first. I could kill him before you get within an arm's length of me, you fai—" His speech was suddenly cut short as the sound of a gunshot cut through the air, catching us all by surprise. The Wraith looked down to see a hole in his body, which had narrowly avoided hitting his hostage, and as he fell to the floor, he released Marek. The source of the gunshot was a federal agent who was sitting in a pool of blood nearby. He held a pistol in one hand while the other was making a futile attempt to stem the flow of blood from a massive wound in his chest. A short glance revealed several deep scratches gouged into his clothes, his eyes going in and out of focus.

"I know what you're thinking," the agent said, coughing. "How the hell did I just pull that one off?"

"You should rest," Selina said, helping him sit up. "We'll get you help; I'm sure we can get you to a medic."

"It's too late for me," the agent said with a sad smile, "but I like to think my body held out long enough to give you this." He handed the gun to Selina. "It appears fairies have tried to communicate with a President before; they may not have persuaded him to convert the world to believing in you again, but he left behind this gun and six enchanted bullets, saying that when the time came we'd know what to do with it." He coughed, closing his eyes and wincing at the pain. "I'm afraid there are only two left, so you'd better be sparing in using it." And then, with one last rattling breath and a slight shake of his body, he went limp.

"We should have tried to heal him," I said, feeling a little shaken by the scale of the carnage inside the building. "He saved our lives and did nothing."

"Our magic isn't limitless, Clint," Nightshade said, placing a hand on my shoulder. "Even the most experienced healer cannot heal all wounds. What matters—"

"Where's Mickey?" Crystal suddenly asked, cutting Nightshade off. "He was here a second ago." Suddenly a scream cut through the air. "That's him!" she cried.

"It's coming from the Oval Office," Selina said, running quickly away from the dead Wraith—so quickly, in fact, that we barely kept pace with her.

We met no more resistance until we reached the famous room, which was empty apart from one of Feth'rael's communication devices, sitting in the middle of the desk in a small pool of blood.

"Please tell me that's not Mickey's blood," Selina said as she ran over and activated the device to reveal an image of Mickey, bleeding wound on his temple lying at Feth'rael's feet. "If he's dead, all the armies of the underworld won't protect you from me, scum!" she spat.

"Such an amusing—if meaningless—threat," Feth'rael said from somewhere off screen with a deep laugh. "You fools played right into my hands! What greater victory than to have those who seek to be the saviors of humans and fairies actually become the hosts of the very beings who will bring about their destruction. If you think you can stop me, the gateway to the ritual is there," he said, extending a holographic hand and pointing to a portal so dark in the barely-lit room we hadn't even noticed it. "Be quick, however, as my children are…hungry…to meet you."

"I'm going after him," Selina growled, grabbing the gun, "I'm not letting him die out there!" She was stopped by Nightshade's hand on her shoulder. "What the hell are you doing?" she snapped at him.

"You cannot fight Feth'rael alone," Nightshade replied. "Take the others with you; I'll make sure no enemy follows you through." For a moment Selina seemed likely to complain, but she knew the older fairy was right. "Good luck to all of you," he said, saluting us, "though I hope you don't require it."

Chapter 25

When we stepped through the portal, we found ourselves on the rocky shoreline of a windswept island, the landscape in front of us dominated by a massive outcrop that looked more akin to a human tower than any natural landmark. As well as myself and Selina there was Crystal, Marek, Nara, and a handful of fairies Nightshade had insisted we take with us. I almost immediately felt underdressed as an especially cold breeze made all my hairs stand on end, the others pulling whatever clothing they had more tightly around them.

"I can't tell whether this is natural weather or some kind of spell," Crystal said, looking at our new surroundings. "Either way, I'm making a mental note never to visit here again."

"I think the weather might be the least of our problems," Nara said, pointing up at the cliff. Several Wraiths—along with some strange, insect-like creatures that were the size of a grown human—were clambering down the cliffs toward us. "Damnit, should've guessed he wouldn't just let us walk straight in there unmolested. There's our way up!" she said, pointing the enchanted blade toward a set of steps. They led up the cliff toward the only visible hole that anything larger than a small bird could enter. "I guess we'll just have to fight our way in then."

"Let's just hope Mickey can hold on long enough for us to get there," Selina said as she threw a small fireball at the first insect to jump off the cliff toward us, burning it instantly. With that, the other creatures jumped almost as one, causing us to scatter to avoid them landing directly on our heads.

While the insects were relatively easy to dispatch, we soon found ourselves caught in a running fight against the Wraiths. Although we were able to avoid them killing us as easily as they had some of their opponents, they still moved quickly enough that landing anything resembling a fatal blow seemed impossible.

"This is no good!" Selina shouted, narrowly avoiding one of the Wraiths slashing her right side with its claws. "He knows we can't win a fight like this; he's just trying to delay us long enough for the ritual to become irreversible."

"She's right," Nara said with a grimace, finding her magic bouncing harmlessly off the Wraith that was rapidly closing the distance to her. "We'll die of old age before we can kill them. We need a new strategy." She dodged a swing of a claw aimed at her head, then nearly jumped out of her skin when there was a sudden gunshot, the Wraith in front of her falling down as she saw I'd pulled out the gun the agent had given us. "As much as I appreciate you using that gun to help," she said, "that leaves us with just one bullet. Don't fire it here—we may need to use it in that chamber before this fight is over."

"I have an idea," Marek said, his voice suddenly deeper than I remembered it being before, "but right now I advise you all to duck and cover your eyes."

We didn't take even a second to ask what he was talking about, and within a moment I felt a sudden, intense heat passing over my back, which dissipated almost as quickly as it had appeared. When I opened my eyes, I saw the burnt remains of Wraiths all around us, my momentary panic being quickly allayed when I saw the others around me, seemingly unharmed by what had just occurred.

At the center of our huddle was Marek, his body glowing as if it was on fire, though he didn't appear in any pain.

As we stood up something suddenly caught my eye, the air around us seeming to shimmer as if caught in the haze of a summer day. What happened next occurred faster than I could comprehend, my eye catching only the briefest glimpse of Feth'rael appearing in our midst before I suddenly lost consciousness, hitting the ground with a thud.

I groaned as I came to, my head feeling as if several piles of bricks had just been dropped on it from a great height, my arms completely immobile.

My feelings weren't too improved when I opened my

eyes to discover I was being held high up on the wall of an immense chamber by what appeared to be spider's silk, but which was so strong I struggled to even fidget against it. Turning my head I saw Selina to one side of me, a cut across her left cheek, while on the other side there were Niana and Crystal. None of them were moving. A quick glance below showed Feth'rael evidently mid-ritual, his hands glowing green, Mickey's motionless body lying in front of him.

Suddenly I heard a groan from nearby, and I turned to see Selina slowly opening her eyes.

"I've had three-day hangovers more pleasant than this," she said, letting out an aggravated grunt as she realized she couldn't move her arm to touch the cut. A look of horror slowly spread across her face as she took in the scene below us. "Oh, this isn't good."

"Can't you just magic us out of these?" Crystal asked groggily, also having just come round. "I feel like they're draining the energy out of me."

"It's not that simple," Selina replied after a hopeless attempt to cast a fire spell. "Whatever this is made out of, it's dampening my magic." She looked at the substance again. "With time and patience I could maybe break through, but we don't have much of either. Plus, all our weapons are down there," she added, nodding toward a pile in one corner of the cavern that was giving off a familiar blue glow. She winced as she tried to shift her position.

"*Clint, we need to talk,*" she seemed to say within my head. "*I'm speaking telepathically in the vain hope Feth'rael can't hear us like this. Have you noticed someone's missing here?"*

"*What do you…*" I trailed off, suddenly realizing what she meant. I thought for a moment. "*Marek? I saw him, after he cast the spell, but after that it's pretty much a blank until I woke up here.*"

"*There's two possibilities,*" she said, grimacing. "*Marek is dead, or he somehow escaped, in which case we can only hope he's somewhere nearby and can actually help us get the hell out of here.*"

"What are we doing here?" Niana shouted at Feth'rael, suddenly cutting through our telepathic conversation. "If you wanted us dead, you would've finished us off."

"How…perceptive…of you," Feth'rael said with a chuckle, turning toward us but leaving the green glow behind him. "My children can possess dead bodies, but it is far more…effective…to gift them living ones. Besides, this way you'll live long enough to see everything your bodies do, while being absolutely powerless to stop it from happening."

"If I'm your child, why give me to them?" Crystal spat. "I'd have thought you'd want me alive to manipulate to your heart's content."

"That was my plan," Feth'rael replied. "Sadly, your mother's human blood appears to have corrupted you, and you cannot be turned to my side willingly. So, I will simply give you no choice in the matter. I should have acted sooner; you pitiful creatures have been corrupted by humanity for so long you would rather protect them than save yourselves, even one whose kin suffered against the British."

"Oh no," Selina said louder than she intended. "Clint, he knows about Marek's parentage."

"You genuinely believe someone could hide that from me?" Feth'rael asked with a laugh. "I always knew who he was; I planned to corrupt him—he and your mother would be the advance guard of my invasion—however, I hadn't realized you would find my hiding place quite so expertly. But, no fear, Marek will turn. I've turned stronger creatures than him to my side; he's only delaying the inevitable."

"If you believe that, then it's not humans or fairies who are the fools," a loud voice echoed around the chamber, it taking us all a second to realize it was Marek's. He stepped into the light, his whole body seemingly surrounded by flames that appeared to leave not one visible scratch on his body. "If you think you can win a fight against me, here I am—let us fight a magical duel like fairies used to."

"You're challenging me?" Feth'rael asked, seeming to grow an extra foot in height as he turned toward Marek. "You couldn't destroy me if you had them!"

"Maybe we should test that theory," Marek said, bringing a fist down against the floor that immediately broke our prisons, freeing us. I was glad we had our wings, even though Crystal and I took a moment to act on instinct and use them, otherwise the drop to the chamber floor may have caused more injuries. "I'm sorry, guys," Marek said, his voice returning to its more familiar tone.

"He placed some kind of hex spell on me to trap me by the shore; it took all my strength to break through it."

"All that matters is you're here now," I said, clenching my fist as I felt the anger rising within me. "Just like the vision said: we're all together to end this, once and for all."

"Oh, this will be the end," Feth'rael chuckled, "but it won't end in your favor." He clapped his hands together then, the burst of green energy it released almost knocking us flat.

As I regained my balance, I was worried to see Niana lying on the floor, motionless. I made to move in her direction.

"She's okay, Clint," Selina shouted as she cast a spell at Feth'rael, who deflected it with alarming ease. "Right now we need to worry about how the hell we're going to fight him!"

"Here," Nara said, levitating the blades she'd managed to reach while the enemy had been distracted. "I don't know if these will have any effect, but I'm not convinced we have many more options."

"I may be able to restrain him," Marek said telepathically, grunting as he narrowly escaped getting hit by a blast of energy. "But you'll have to distract him—us attacking him one by one is making it too easy for him to block our attacks."

"But how do we—" I started saying, before a chance glance at the cavern's ceiling provided some much-needed inspiration. "Well, here goes nothing," I muttered under my breath, starting to whisper a spell I had no idea how I'd learned before slamming my hand down into the dirt.

At first, nothing seemed to have happened.

"The fae placed their trust in *you*?" Feth'rael asked, letting out a loud laugh of disbelief. "That didn't even come close to hurting—"

He stopped as we all heard a loud rumble coming from the ceiling above, and as a large stalactite from far above fell, Feth'rael barely moved out of the way in time before finding something was holding him in place. It only took a moment for us to identify the source. Marek was bending down on one knee with his hand outstretched, while a highly visible white glow that had appeared around his body now surrounded Feth'rael as well.

"Someone do something!" Marek hissed, his voice strained. "He's fighting the binding spell! I can't hold this forever, and if he breaks it, I'm not sure the same trick will work twice!"

"We can't!" Nara exclaimed as the rest of us realized we were as unable to move as Feth'rael was. "He may not be mobile but he's still casting spells. I don't know anything that could break this!"

Suddenly there was a loud crack, followed by an almost supernatural groan from Feth'rael. A gunshot wound was suddenly showing through his cloak, his thick black blood spilling from it. As he looked down at the wound, Feth'rael's eyes widened. "What? What did you do?"

He attempted to move toward us in spite of the spell—his face a picture of agony—before vanishing in a blast of light that freed us from our own bonds.

We turned around to see Mickey, propped up on one elbow, the gun we'd been given in one of his hands.

Selina was the first to run over to him. "I thought you were dead!" she cried, pulling him into a tight hug before releasing her grip slightly when he winced. "You pull that crap again and I'll kill you myself!" she added, though she was smiling.

"Thanks?" Mickey said, letting out a nervous laugh that was cut short by Selina suddenly kissing him. It only lasted for a moment before she let go of him again, her blushes saved by our approach. "Please tell me this is over," Mickey said, his own face going rather red now too, "I quite like the sound of being the one who saved the world."

"We shouldn't get too ahead of ourselves," Marek warned us. "The danger hasn't passed entirely—you need to see this."

We turned to see that, while all sign of the enemy had vanished, the portal was still open, and now it was expanding.

"I thought the portal would close once he was dead," I said, my voice barely more than a whisper.

"There are two important pieces of information you're unaware of, Clint," Selina said, panic rising in her voice. "One, whatever he truly is, I'm not convinced it's possible to actually kill Feth'rael outright—in all likelihood we've simply banished him back to wherever he came from—and two, killing him probably would've had no effect anyway. There's only one way to close those portals," she said, pausing as she closed her eyes, "and that has to be done from the other side."

"But that would trap someone on the other side," Crystal said angrily. "Who the hell's going to volunteer to do that?"

"I will," Marek said so suddenly it caught the rest of us off guard. "You all have families and lives to return to; we wouldn't even be here if I hadn't helped him build the portals."

"Like hell am I letting you do that," Crystal said, probably more angrily than she'd intended. "No, we *will* find another way."

"You don't need to—I'll do it," said a voice from the direction of the tunnel we'd used to enter the chamber. We were surprised to see Nightshade enter, but even more so to see how suddenly unhealthy he looked. "You all have your whole lives ahead of you; it is not your place to give your lives here."

"I don't understand," Crystal said, stepping toward him. "Why would you do this? And what happened to you?"

"I'm dying," Nightshade replied. "I have been for some time. Whatever the cause of my illness, no fairy magic or remedy has been able to do more than simply delay the inevitable." He sighed, shaking his head. "I hid it because Nareena needed to believe she had my strength to support her in the darkest times. I finally told her, however, before we departed for this battle, also telling her I had loved her since we were children being taught by her great aunt and that I was scared to leave her alone." He looked down at the ground, apparently overcome with emotion. "She told me that she'd long known I loved her, and that whatever happened she would never be alone. She told me to do whatever it took to ensure we won, and that if I was to die here then I was to know she would never forget me. None of my kin would ever forget what I did."

"We're not letting you die," Crystal said, hugging him before he could say a word to stop her. "Too many people have died because of this damned war already."

"My fate is already sealed, child," he said, shaking his head. "I am a warrior; if I am allowed to choose how I die I would rather die helping protect this world than withering away in a bed, forcing the only woman I ever loved to watch me slowly fade away." He smiled at Crystal, who was crying now. "I can, however, do one last thing for you all." He walked over to Niana, kneeling next to her unconscious form and placing something wrapped in a leaf against her chest, which glowed briefly before spreading to her body and dissipating quickly. "She will recover. Now, you must go, I have a strong feeling you don't want to be here when this portal shuts."

"But..." I could feel myself hesitating even as I found the words dying on my lips, and in the end, we simply hugged him in turn, Nightshade surprising us by returning the hugs willingly.

Then, with one last look we ran out of the cave, all of us feeling the tears beginning to flow.

We stumbled back through the portal into the Oval Office,

most of us still in too much shock to register Selina's quick spell that shut the portal behind us. The sounds of battle could still be heard outside, the room being lit by the glow of fires all around the lawn outside.

Suddenly the sky was filled with a sudden burst of eerie green light, which lit the area more intensely than even the strongest sunlight ever could.

"It's...it's done," Selina said, no longer hiding her tears. "I sense the portals are closed. I just...wish..."

Mickey pulled her into a hug, allowing her to cry on his shoulder. The others slumped to the floor as the sounds of battle around the building slowly faded into silence.

"Well, at least we can go home," I said, walking over to the desk at the center of the room. "After this I think we all deserve a nice long—" Suddenly, without any warning, I felt light-headed, and before I even knew what was happening, I started falling, losing consciousness long before my body hit the floor.

Chapter 26

It was the strangely calming whistling sound that finally made me start coming round. It was relaxing enough, and for a moment I began to wonder if everything I'd just experienced had all been a dream and that I'd open my eyes to my mother telling me I'd be late for school.

It was the scent of sea air that dispelled this pleasant thought—after all, my house was at least twenty minutes' drive from the sea.

As I slowly opened my eyes, I found myself staring up at a ceiling that appeared to have been painted to resemble a cloudy sky, and as I took in the odd pattern above me, my last memories began flooding back.

"Niana!" I said, sitting bolt upright in the camp bed I was lying in, pain shooting up my right arm as I did so. "I need to find her, make sure she's okay."

I felt a gentle but insistent hand pushing me back onto the bed, revealed to be Selina, a pair of delicate reading glasses perched on her nose and a book held in one hand. I allowed her to help me lie back on a raised pillow.

"Where's Niana?"

"She's sleeping," Selina replied. "She came round long before you and insisted on staying by your side, but I told her she needed sleep so she could recover from her own injuries." She smiled. "All things considered, however, the end result could have been far worse."

"What happened?" I asked. "I mean, after I blacked out."

"We won," Selina said with a sigh. "With the portals closed a large number of the enemy's monsters simply vanished—presumably they could only maintain their presence here as long as Feth'rael remained in the mortal world. Those left behind who hadn't been killed either fled or surrendered; apparently without their leader they soon lost any interest in fighting." She paused for a moment, looking down at her hands. "Sadly, there were casualties on our side as well. Do you remember the soldier we met in New York who offered whatever help his unit could provide?"

"Of course," I said, trying to be optimistic at first before I realized her eyes were red from crying. "Oh no, what happened?"

"It appears offering to help us made his base a target," she replied. "Feth'rael sent a force to attack the nearby town, and the division did what they could to defend it while evacuating civilians. They came across a bus full of schoolchildren in the path of a pack of Fenrir, immediately worrying about getting the kids clear. Unfortunately, the soldier was killed just before the task was completed; his last action was pushing a young woman in a wheelchair clear just before the Fenrir reached the bus. The US Senate are already talking about fast-tracking a posthumous Medal of Honor for him, and I don't think anyone will object, all things considered."

I lay there silently for a moment as I took in all this new information. "Where am I?" I asked after a while.

"Now *that's* an interesting story," Selina said with a wry smile. "When you collapsed, we knew you needed immediate medical attention, but Ressik's forces were too busy tending to their own dead and injured for us to feel comfortable asking them for aid. Seeing how upset Crystal was, Nara decided it was well past time for the Pixie Queen to do as her daughter asked, so she brought us to Cornwall and essentially threatened to never speak to her mother again if she didn't allow us entry. Thankfully we were allowed to enter." She smiled. "You're in one of the rooms of the Tower of Healing in the great Pixie Enclave, somewhere near the town of St. Austell. When you feel well enough you should go outside; the English coast are incredible. I'm not gonna lie, I'd love to have grown up against a cliff with blue seas and quaint villages as far as the eye can see"

"Hopefully I'll be able to do that sooner or later," I said, trying to turn over and feeling the shot of pain again. "Okay, I should've asked this before, but I don't remember getting attacked that violently, so how come I blacked out?" I winced. "Why am I in this much pain?"

"It appears the two spells Feth'rael used on us had more of an effect than we'd initially felt," Selina explained. "My guess is that adrenaline had been coursing through our bodies, although in your case I think it's partly due to your overuse of magic. Young fairies are taught, as soon as they start learning magic for the first time, to use it sparingly. It requires considerable amounts of energy to use regularly, and as amusing as even I find this, we teenagers don't have as much energy as we like to believe we do. You have a few cuts and bruises, but—much to your girlfriend's delight—you'll live." She couldn't help laughing at the shade of red my face had suddenly turned at the mention of Niana. "Oh, and I have some news to give you about my...situation. After everything that happened, having come so close to never seeing him again, I decided my father deserved the truth."

"What did he say?" I asked, smiling at her for her courage.

"He said he'd always known there was something different about me," she replied, her voice wobbling slightly with the emotion. "Even though he couldn't quite put a finger on what it was. Then he said he didn't care who I wanted to be, that I was his child and he would support me in whatever I wanted to do with my life. He also said that if anyone treated me differently because of who I am—or who I will be—they'd have him to answer to." She took a moment to take a deep breath before continuing. "Then he hugged me tighter than he has since I was a little girl and just held me for quite a while."

"I told you he'd be fine with it," I said, smiling again. "I don't always talk nonsense, you know."

"I know," she replied, placing her hand on mine. "I wouldn't have been able to tell him the truth at all if you hadn't said what you did that night, so thank you." She leaned over, kissing my forehead softly. "The other news is pretty big, or at least, I think so anyway. I've met someone." She let out a soft laugh. "Well, I say *met*...it was someone I already knew. And before you ask, no it's not that asshole from Fort Knox—all the money and alcohol on the planet couldn't persuade me to find him attractive."

"But then who could..." I started saying, before my eye was drawn to the jewellery around her neck. "It's Mickey, isn't it?"

"Is it that obvious?" Selina asked, letting out a giggle. "Was it me kissing him in the heat of battle that gave it away?"

"That was confirmation you liked him," I replied, laughing too, "but, no, the giveaway was that necklace you're wearing. I was there the day his grandmother gave it to him, when she made him promise he'd keep it until he found someone special to give it to. Am I allowed to ask how this happened?"

"Well, it started with Mickey fainting from blood loss," Selina replied. "Yeah," she added upon seeing my expression, "his problem was easier to diagnose than yours. Before he lost consciousness, when I'd been quick enough for him to avoid hitting the floor too hard, he told me he loved me. I wanted it to be true—much as I half expected it just to be shock—so once I was sure the rest of you were safe I took a chair by his bed." She paused, clearly remembering. "It was on the second night of my vigil when, half asleep, I heard him say we needed to talk. So, the next morning, we sat and talked. I was honest with him, expecting…who I am…to put him off, but he said we weren't so different; we were both trying to discover who we were. He told me he'd fallen for me the moment he saw me, and that, if I wanted, we could find out who we were meant to be together. I know, it's a shock," she finished.

"Not at all," I said, smiling broadly. "All I want is for my friends to be happy, and judging by your smile, you two are." Before I could say any more, or before Selina could offer a response, the door to the room suddenly opened and Niana stepped inside, dressed in a simple green floral dress, with a ring of flowers around her head. Seeing me awake she ran over, hugging me hard enough that I winced slightly, causing her to release her grip.

"I'm sorry," she said, wiping a tear from her eye. "You've been unconscious for so long, I…I feared the worst."

"I did too," I said, gently brushing her cheek. "Somehow, seeing you unmoving on the floor was scarier than facing the lord of the fairy underworld in a fight." I kissed her then, amused to see how pink she turned. "Why do I get the feeling you aren't just here to check up on me?"

"You're right," she replied, giving an embarrassed laugh. "Elion has returned for a brief…I suppose you could call it a 'debrief', but also because he's offering us a chance to speak to the loved ones we've lost in this war. He allowed me to speak with my mother, it…well, it may not have repaired all the damage that's been done, but it ensured that I'm at peace with what passed between us, for the first time in a long time. He's offering you that chance too."

"I'd like that," I said, trying to hide a note of sadness in my voice. "Could you come with me? They didn't have a chance to meet you properly before."

"Of course," she said, smiling. "Rest, now—we'll come back for you soon enough."

I was uncertain how much time had passed before I felt something brush against my hand, and when I opened my eyes, I found Niana looking down at me, though this time the entire room seemed to be white. I sat up, feeling surprised at seeing my mother and father standing a short distance away, before remembering the conversation from before. I stood up, walking over to them as they pulled me into a group hug, which felt far more solid than I had expected, the comfort of their arms around me mixing me with both joy and fresh grief, and then invited Niana to join us as she was standing awkwardly to one side.

"I'm sorry," I said, crying. "I should've saved you; there must've been something I could've done."

"You couldn't have done more than you did, Clint," my father said, pulling back slightly, lifting my chin so I would look into his eyes. "Elion told us what you did, what you were willing to do to save people you didn't even know. I've always been proud of you, and you've simply proven to me now why I feel such pride looking at you."

"I should be apologizing to you," my mother said. "I

shouldn't have hidden who you were from you, that was wrong. I don't blame you if you're angry with me; I know I would be in your position."

"I'm not angry," I said, smiling. "I was at first, but with everything that's happened...everything I've seen...I understand why you wanted to protect me. Besides, you've given me a pretty amazing pair of wings," I added, allowing them to unfurl behind me and enjoying hearing my parents laugh again. "I'm not sure I'm ready to let you go, though—I can't lose you from my life."

"You aren't losing us," my father said, kneeling down in front of me. "We'll always be with you in spirit, and now we know that we'll see each other again one day. Besides, you have a beautiful young lady to look after you now." I didn't need to see Niana's face to know she'd turned a deep red at the comment. "Before you go," he said, reaching into his pocket and taking out something wrapped in his favorite handkerchief, "this is for you. I promise you'll know what to do with it when the time comes."

"Thank you," I said, pocketing the object without giving a second's thought as to what it might be. "I guess we'd better go," I said, hugging them again. "If I ever find a way to reach you again, I will. I love you both."

"We love you too," my father said, my mother crying too much to speak. "Now go, and make us—and both your heritages—proud." As I let them go, they vanished, leaving me and Niana alone in the white space.

For a moment I stared at the empty space where they had stood, fresh tears threatening to fall.

Niana stepped closer to me. "C'mon," she said, taking my hand. "We need to go see the others; I'm sure Crystal and Mickey would be glad to see you up and about again."

Once we'd returned to reality, Niana led me through a series of corridors, each of which were plainly decorated, except for the occasional strange painting. We passed many doors, from which the occasional noise emanated, but other than that we saw no sign of life within the building at all.

We eventually reached a large, oak door, which Niana opened onto a scene so bright it took me a moment for my eyesight to adjust enough to see anything.

I couldn't help but gasp as I caught my first glimpse of the Pixie colony: it stretched out as far as the eye could see, from small, one-bedroom houses to buildings that looked like the fairy equivalent of a shopping mall. At the far end of the city was a tree that towered over it all, its branches offering the city below at least some protection from the hot summer sunshine. Among the streets I could see fairies of all kinds milling around, talking and sharing food, but I was more surprised to see human soldiers among them, only identifiable by their uniforms as their weapons were nowhere to be seen.

After allowing me to take in the scenery for a moment Niana took me over to a set of steps set into the side of the tower that led down to a platform about halfway down. Before I could take in the group waiting for me Crystal rushed over, nearly knocking me off my feet as she gave me a bear hug, then letting out an embarrassed laugh as she heard me wince.

"Thank god you're okay," Crystal said, a mix of anger and relief in her voice. "You've nearly died on me twice in one month—you pull that stunt again and I'll smack you until you wake up, you hear me?"

"Nice to see you too," I replied, laughing as she hugged me again. I smiled at Mickey, who was sitting with Selina on his lap, her head resting on his shoulder. "Glad to see you smiling again, Mickey."

"I hear I have you to thank for that, at least in part," he said. "You gave her the confidence to be honest with everyone; not sure I'd have had the guts to tell her myself."

"Well, at least some good came of all this," I said, trying to suppress a chuckle. "My two best friends are both all loved up for once."

"Not just your friends, Mickey," came my Uncle Nick's voice from somewhere behind me. I turned to see him, dressed in a well-pressed tuxedo, leading Nareena—herself in a green dress that seemed to shimmer like a rainbow as the sun hit it—down to the platform. It only took me a moment to see the large ring on her finger. Selina's father was following at a short distance behind. "You had us all worried, kid," Nick said, giving me a gentler hug than the one Crystal had given me. "I'm not sure your parents would've given me a good night's sleep ever again if I'd let something happen to you."

"You didn't *let* me do anything," I said, more humorously than out of any anger. "My mum realizes you've fallen in love with another fairy?"

"I..." He stopped for a moment, his evident embarrassment causing all the others to let out a chuckle. "The ring was your mother's idea," he said once he'd regained his composure. "She said that if this should teach me anything it should be to hold on to what you care about, because you don't know when it might be taken from you. I don't know if she was actually telling me to propose, but I certainly had the urge to. Frankly, I was amazed the Queen even said yes."

"It was something Nightshade said to me," Nareena admitted. "Elion allowed me one last chance to speak to him, and he looked more peaceful than I've seen him in...well, in a long time," she said, wiping a tear from her cheek. "I told him I didn't know what I'd do without his guidance and protection, and he said I didn't need him, because there was one who would offer me all that if I would just be brave enough to say yes. And, as you humans say, the rest is history."

"Anything else you guys want to catch me up on?" I asked, raising an eyebrow. "I'm beginning to think I was out for the count for more than three days...maybe start with why there's a load of human soldiers walking around a city I didn't even know existed two weeks ago?"

"They're here for two reasons," Nareena replied. "Partly so they can be offered whatever medical aid they require, but also because the leaders of your world have decided that the fact humans and fairies have discovered each other once again deserves a great celebration. Besides, we must all begin to plan for the future."

"What do you mean?" I asked.

"Well, once the Queen convinced the world leaders that with Feth'rael banished a peace treaty was unnecessary, it was decided it was time to put the relationship on a more…formal basis," Nick replied. "All countries asked if they could send their own envoys to ensure good relations. The PM was glad to hear about me and the Queen—apparently I was the only person he could think of appropriate for the job. Besides, I'm not going to pass up the chance for more time with my wife-to-be."

"America is gonna be a bit more interesting," Selina said, watching her father. "It seems Feth'rael murdered the vice-president when he presumably outgrew his usefulness, which ordinarily would see the Speaker of the House take control, but…"

"I'm going to be restored to the job as soon as I'm done here. It turns out when you play a part in saving the world it makes you rather popular with everyone," her father said with an embarrassed laugh. "I wanted at the very least to have an election, but the Republicans made it pretty clear they wouldn't put anyone up to oppose me, and no one else is either willing or able to do so."

"What about the rest of us?" Crystal asked. "Much as I like this place, it's gonna feel like we're imposing on the Pixies if we just stay here indefinitely."

"We won't be staying here forever," Nareena replied. "Once I was certain the fighting had finished, I sent scouts to retrieve those survivors of the Glade who hadn't joined the fight and to bring them here. We'll stay here for a short time, but we plan on rebuilding the Shadow Glade, though this time with a name that reflects the new era of hope we live in. Marek and his uncle will come with us; we have strong suspicions the answers to his heritage may lie within the old archives somewhere. As for the rest of you, that is your choice to make, but there's a place for you among the fairies if you wish."

"I'm going with Nara," Crystal said. "Her mother has apparently woken from her metaphorical slumber and decided the Pixies need to reconnect with their fellow fairies. Nara pretty much threatened to never speak to her again if she wasn't allowed to be her envoy to the Glade. This way I can finish my studies but still get to be with her."

"Me and Selina are joining the new city too," Mickey said. "Us three are orphans now, Clint; this way we can still study, see our family, and get to know our new heritage at last."

"Your dad is okay with this?" I asked Selina, raising an eyebrow.

"You're assuming I gave him a choice," she replied, laughing, looking towards her father, who gave her a warm smile. "But no, he's fine with it—I've never studied in a proper school so it's not like many will notice I've gone, and I can teleport home whenever I want to. Besides, there's not much about American fairies I don't already know; this way I can spend time with Mickey and find out what the fairies this side of the Atlantic are really like."

"You don't have to join us," Niana said, squeezing my hand gently. "I would do anything to have you there but I'm not going to stop you spending time with Nick or your other family—"

"In all fairness, I'm gonna be seeing a lot of Nick," I said with a laugh. "My mother would never let me hear the end of it if the girl I loved was offering me a home and I rejected it without good reason." As she moved to kiss me, my mind wandered to the item in my pocket, and I reached my hand in to take it out. It only took a single touch of the object for me to realise what it was, and why my father had given it to me. "I'm probably about to make a complete fool of myself, so nobody laugh," I said. "I know I'm still a kid but...what Nick said was right, you have to keep hold of those you care about." I began to take it out of my pocket before Niana stopped me.

"Yes," she said, smiling sweetly. "The only answer I could possibly give is yes."

"But how do you know what I'm going to ask?" I asked, feeling confused.

"I don't need Selina's or my sister's telepathy skills to know," she replied, taking my hand out and opening it to reveal a small but beautiful golden ring with a glimmering blue gem at its centre. "I wasn't entirely honest about what Elion showed me; your mother wanted to speak to me too. She told me what your father planned to give you, and said it was my choice what my answer was, but that I'd meet few young men as loyal as you." She kissed me again. "I knew that already, so my mind was made up long before you even knew you wanted to ask me."

"Well, a double wedding is gonna be a joy to try and organize," Nick said, as he and Nareena hugged us, the others walking over to congratulate us as well. "And that's without even figuring out how the hell to sort out the guest list."

"We can worry about that when the celebration is done, my love," Nareena said, flashing him a smile broader than I'd seen her give anyone in the entire time I'd known her. "We should enjoy this peace; I doubt it will last forever."

"Maybe," I said, looking around at my friends and to the expanse of the city beyond the platform, "but at least with our two species working together again, we should be ready for whatever comes next."

Niana smiled at me. "That we will."

Epilogue

During the attack by Feth'rael, Mike Thomas had been on leave from his security job at a psychiatric hospital, enjoying a holiday with his family. In fact, his mind was still so wrapped up in holiday mode that he only realized he had company when his colleague, Carlos, buzzed himself into the security office.

"Is your mind still on the beach, Mike?" Carlos asked, grinning.

"If it's a choice between the warm Florida sun and a cold security office in Nowheresville, Idaho, can you blame me?" Mike asked with a wry smile. "Although, after three days of the boys telling me how wonderful the fairies on TV were I was kind of glad to get back here."

"Not the same without you here, man," Carlos said as he took a sip from his bottle of water, looking at the clock on the wall. "Shouldn't you be patrolling right now?"

"Crap," Mike exclaimed, getting out of his chair and

grabbing one of the walkie-talkies. "Good thing you reminded me."

"See you in a bit, bud!" Carlos called after Mike as he walked out the door.

"Don't get too comfortable, Carlos!" Mike called back just as the door closed.

He began his patrol down the corridor, past relatively peaceful rooms; most of the patients were either asleep, reading a book, or watching television. In fact, the patients were always so relaxed and peaceful that he and Carlos often wondered what had caused them to be referred in the first place, although as no more than a mere security guard he knew his opinion would matter little to the professionals.

He'd almost made it to the end of the first corridor without incident when he stopped outside the final door. Strange noises were emanating from within, and when he opened the door he reached for his walkie-talkie. "Carlos, the patient in room twelve, is she supposed to have writing tools?"

"Oh, you weren't here, were you?" Carlos replied. "The professor said she could as long as they weren't sharp objects; allowing her to indulge her creative side might help her recovery." There were a few moments of silence. "Is something wrong, Mike?"

"No, not at all," Mike replied, watching for a moment before shaking his head, closing the door, and walking into the next section of rooms.

Room twelve contained only one occupant: a teenage girl with curly ginger hair who had indeed put her writing tools to good use. Covering huge swathes of the walls were the same four words written repeatedly, in various sizes:

The Ravens Are Coming

The Ravens Are Coming

The Ravens Are Coming

Acknowledgements

Thank you to my family, especially my Mum, for keeping my spirits up when yet another rejection had shaken my belief that my books would see the light of day; my Dad for helping take the initial written version and set it on the path toward publication; friends like Sarah for tolerating me droning on about my latest crazy plot idea that might never see the light of day; Jake for giving me a nudge to consider a story idea that didn't even have a name at the time.

I also owe a debt to some of my university tutors: Sam North, for leading me to read the book that ultimately inspired me starting to write *Fairy War*; Alison Habens for being my dissertation supervisor helping the early chapters to begin to take more shape; Steven O'Brien for inspiring the Irish section of the story, perhaps a little ironic since fantasy is not a genre he enjoys.

Last, but by no means least: RJ Anderson, an author who went from someone I was unfamiliar with to a favourite author whose stories helped shape the world of the Fae Age; Jessica Grace Coleman for taking a very rough draft and turning it into a more presentable book; Craig and John at Deep Hearts for taking a punt and not running away at a pitch for a trilogy.

About E.J. Graham

EJ is an avid gamer, reader and comic book movie fan, who belongs to more fandoms than can be counted. When they're not geeking out over the newest Marvel movie they can be found writing one of their many stories, in the case of Fairy War one that has been planned since university.

More From Deep Hearts YA

The Mixtape to My Life
Jake Martinez

Justin has always been comfortable in his skin, even if the world around him wasn't. A junior simply counting down the days for when he can leave for college, Justin's life is thrown for a loop when the one thing that helps him feel like himself suddenly slips away from him. But an unexpected blast from his past puts summer on a new and exciting path, one as random and unexpected as a mixtape.

Squishy Crushy Something
Kieran Frank

Jayden never expected he'd be the type to develop a squish on a boy, never mind a full-blown crush. But now he has two.

L.I.F.E.
Felyx Lawson

Rider is a closeted high school student and would be happy to stay that way, if not for two obstacles in his path: an assignment about love, and Cameron Walker, a new student who is so much more than the jock he first appears to be.

More From Deep Hearts YA

Mark of Ravage and Ruin
Jacyn Gormish
Trapped in the Asylum and destined to become an assassin, Barli wants nothing more than to escape and return to the arms of her girlfriend. But when the moment arises for possible freedom, she learns that a friend is to be killed—and only Barli can save him.

Gerald Ribbon and the Bird in His Brain
Maxwell Bauman
Gerald Ribbon has a habit of ruining his love life, and the bird in his brain that gives him terrible advice certainly isn't helping.

Gay Love and Other Fairy Tales
Dylan James
For football captain Benjamin and his secret boyfriend, cheer co-captain Jordan, there's only one thing standing in the way of their love—Ben's intense need to stay closeted, a need that just might tear them apart.

Deep Hearts YA publishes LGBTQ+ young adult fiction.

Please follow us on social media or
visit our website to find out more.

Instagram: instagram.com/DeepHeartsYA
Twitter: twitter.com/DeepHeartsYA
Facebook: facebook.com/DeepHeartsYA
Website: deepheartsya.com

Printed in Great Britain
by Amazon

12486379R00160